The Dead Beat

Doug Johnstone

W F HOWES LTD

This large print edition published in 2014 by
W F Howes Ltd
Unit 4, Rearsby Business Park, Gaddesby Lane,
Rearsby, Leicester LE7 4YH

1 3 5 7 9 10 8 6 4 2

First published in the United Kingdom in 2014
by Faber & Faber Limited

A CIP catalogue record for this book is available
from the British Library

ISBN 978 1 47127 641 5

Typeset by Palimpsest Book Production Limited,
Falkirk, Stirlingshire

Print... ...in
by TJ In... ...rnwall

For Tricia

'If you're so special, why aren't you dead?'
The Breeders, 'I Just Wanna Get Along'

CHAPTER 1

Martha was surrounded by death.

She swallowed, trying to work up some saliva as she walked through the graveyard. She knew where she was headed. A bluster of wind made the leaves on the oaks rustle as the traffic noise from Portobello Road over the wall receded.

She'd lived ten minutes from Piershill Cemetery her whole life, but it had barely made a blip on her radar until last week. Her dad's funeral.

The cemetery was huge, much bigger than there seemed to be room for in this forgotten corner of Edinburgh. The noman's land between Meadowbank and Portobello, the dead zone that didn't seem to be part of the city's consciousness, just a suburban sprawl round the back of Arthur's Seat, a pebble-dashed dream divvied up into slices with anonymous names like Northfield, Mountcastle, Abercorn. And Duddingston, her own neck of the woods.

She walked past the old gravestones, heading for the newer, shinier plots. The grave markers got smaller and cheesier as she went, corny carvings of old men fishing or angels fluttering. Puky stuff. More fresh flowers as she went on and some other

1

crap too, handwritten notes, a pair of worn slippers, a couple of cans of Tennent's and a half bottle of rum at one grave.

She read the inscriptions as she went past, and worked out the age that each person had been when they died. Eighty-seven, sixty-two, thirty-nine. Dead person bingo. The old-timers, fine. Twenties and thirties, ah well. One teenager, that made her think. She was older than a corpse.

She walked past a gravestone with a carved baby elephant sleeping at the bottom. Looked at the inscription. 'Our Wee Angel, Gemma Marie Davis, Born to Live on a Star'. Checked the dates. Three days old.

Martha took a deep breath and moved on.

And then there he was. Her dad. Simple grey granite slab. 'Ian Lamb'. No 'devoted husband' or 'loving father'. Just the name and the dates. 1970–2014. Forty-four years old. Younger than most in here, but still. Old enough to have two grown kids he hardly ever saw.

There was a bunch of yellow carnations at the foot of the gravestone, already battered by the elements and wilted. She crouched down and fingered the stems, looking for a card. Nothing. She stood up, cricked her neck and rolled her shoulders. Stepped up to the stone and kicked it.

'You arsehole,' she said.

She scuffed at the earth over the grave. There was grass seed scattered on top of the dirt, but it hadn't bedded in yet.

She sighed. 'You stupid coward.'

She hadn't attended the funeral last week. Well, that wasn't strictly true. She'd been so furious with him that she'd worried she might break open his coffin and strangle his corpse in front of everyone. So she'd turned up late and hung about at the other end of the graveyard, the Jewish bit, lurking between gravestones like something out of a Hammer Horror, watching proceedings from a safe distance, not engaging with anyone.

There had only been half a dozen people there. She couldn't make out any of their faces from where she hid amongst the Hebrew carvings and Stars of David, but she knew anyway that she didn't know any of them. Probably just a handful of colleagues. Elaine hadn't gone. Calvin hadn't gone. He had no other family. She didn't know anything else about his life. She only knew about his death, and maybe the circumstances around that were why so few people had gone to his funeral.

She'd waited until the ceremony was over and everyone had left. She walked round the cemetery, circling closer, but didn't go to his grave. She couldn't. She found herself back at the Jewish end, tracing her fingers along the strange, backward writing she couldn't fathom. She left without visiting him that day.

But she was here now.

She looked around. The cemetery was flanked on two sides by busy roads. A number 5 bus went past along Northfield Broadway, the punters on

3

the top deck gazing out in their own little dream worlds.

The rest of the graveyard was surrounded by the same 1960s semi-detached breezeblock houses that were everywhere around here. Just about affordable slivers of homespun happiness. It must be cool, she thought, to have hundreds of dead bodies buried out the back of your home. How would it feel to wake up every morning, open the curtains and spy that mass of human decay? She noticed barbed wire running along the tops of the fences adjoining the cemetery. To keep the vandals out, or the zombies in?

Along the path, two men in overalls were unloading gardening tools from the back of a flatbed truck. The everyday job of maintaining the dead. She turned back to her dad.

'What am I supposed to do now?' She raised her eyebrows. 'Well?'

She pictured the end of *Carrie*, the hand rising out the dirt. She had watched it one night drunk with Cal, cosying into her brother at the scary bits, both of them laughing when she jumped. They'd watched that the same night as *Pet Sematary*, a Stephen King double bill. Cal was the horror fan, Martha just liked the company. She wondered if there was a pet cemetery around here. She could bury Ian there and have him reanimated as an evil, decomposing killer.

She hunkered down by the grave again, stared at the ground. She wanted to see something, a sign.

A wood pigeon flapped down and began pecking at the grass seed she'd kicked up. Almost close enough to grab its neck. Its glassy eyes were oblivious to her as it strutted across her father's fresh grave. She thought about the bullshit of reincarnation. Maybe the wood pigeon would eat the grass seed and fly off, imbued with the spirit of Ian, the selfish, moronic spirit of her dead dad.

She stood up and the wood pigeon flustered into the sky.

'Well, today's the day,' she said to the gravestone. 'You remember, right? You arranged it. My big chance at the *Standard*. Follow in Daddy's footsteps and all that.'

Her tone was aggressive, sarcastic.

She unbuttoned her coat and held it open to show off the maroon blouse and neat black skirt.

'Look, I even dressed like a grown-up.'

With the tights and shoes she felt weird, not the jeans, T-shirts and Cons she was used to. But it also felt good, somehow. Empowering, like she was a real woman.

She buttoned her coat and walked away from the grave, heading for the exit, purpose in her stride. As she crunched down the path, the wood pigeon coo-cooed at her from the branches of an oak. She smiled and doffed a pretend hat towards it.

'Fuck you,' she said to the bird.

CHAPTER 2

Across the road from the bus stop two guys in Kappa stood outside the chemist, swigging methadone from tiny plastic cups. They walked to the empty playpark, slouched onto the swings and stared at Martha.

She turned away and looked for her bus. She dug into her satchel, felt around, then pulled it out. A brick-red Sony Walkman, scraped around the edges, thick black buttons up the side, a built-in microphone at the top. The cassette player she'd liberated from Ian's flat on the day of the funeral. She'd looked it up, it was first produced in 1990, three years before she was born.

A teenage mum with a toddler in a Hibs top was waiting for a bus. She stared at the Walkman.

'Where did you find that relic?'

Martha shrugged. 'It's my dead father's. Got a problem?'

The girl pulled her son to the other end of the bus stop.

Martha rummaged in her bag, her hand rattling around the cassette boxes inside. She grabbed one and eased the tape out, flipped the lid on the Walkman and put the tape in. She plugged her earphones into the socket and pressed the chunky Play button. Two seconds of fuzz and crackle then a burst of guitar riff, drums and bass clattering in after. She looked at the cassette box. *It's a Shame about Ray* by The Lemonheads on side A, *Last Splash* by The Breeders on the other side. Neither meant anything to her. She'd look them up later. She was listening to The Lemonheads. Sounded good, kind of slack.

This was like an archaeological dig, listening to stuff Ian was into before she was born. Stuff he might've listened to with Elaine, when they were together as young lovers. Maybe they went to see The Lemonheads or The Breeders live. Maybe they smoked grass beforehand, slammed tequilas later and danced all night. She tried to imagine her mum as a young woman.

She still held the cassette box in her hand. The track listing was written by hand on the TDK insert card in untidy block capitals. She slid it out and rubbed her thumb over the ink. Tried to comprehend a time before she existed.

The bus arrived. She got on and sat upstairs. The Lemonheads were singing about a ship without a rudder.

She thought about being at Ian's flat. After loitering at the cemetery she'd headed straight for Broughton Street, to The Basement where Cal worked. He was only doing the day shift, so she drank and kept him company, then he joined her at the other side of the bar when he finished.

Things got messy, as always. They argued, as usual.

Cal didn't get his sister's obsession with their biological dad. Ian hadn't played any part in their lives growing up, so who the hell cared? Martha couldn't explain it, but she needed more than that.

She and Cal never agreed on anything, but she loved him to death.

Twins.

She dwelt on the past, Cal thought only about the present. She was motivated for the future, Cal drifted through life. She was straight, he was gay. She was short, he was tall, she was curvy, he was stocky. She was plain, he was beautiful. Cal would argue it the other way, but he was wrong.

And they dealt with their depression in opposite ways. Soon after diagnosis as thirteen-year-olds, Cal was sorted on medication and counselling. Martha hadn't settled on anything for years, yo-yoing in and out of darkness, the brutal, life-sapping crush of it. Until ECT last year. A few minutes under anaesthetic, a recharging of the batteries, and boom, she was back on solid ground. Which reminded her, she had sessions coming later this week.

Couldn't come soon enough. Everything with Ian and the work experience placement was pressing down on her, making it difficult to breathe. She tried to think of the relaxation thing she'd learned, but it was just breathing, right? How hard could it be to breathe? Very, it turned out.

After The Basement closed that night they'd

walked to the spot where it happened, North Bridge, on Martha's insistence.

Cal wasn't impressed. 'This is sick, Munchkin.'

Martha stood on the east side of the bridge looking out. The Firth of Forth was flanked by Calton Hill and Arthur's Seat. A lighthouse blinking somewhere out there. She looked straight down at Waverley Station. The workmen had been at it for years. She noticed that the glass roof nearest to the bridge had been replaced by metal.

She couldn't see properly, so she hoisted herself up onto the wall of the bridge.

'Hey,' Cal said. 'What are you doing?'

She looked at him. 'It's OK, I'm not my father's daughter.'

Nevertheless he stood next to her, his hand at her back, ready to grab her.

She looked down again and realised. This was the best place to jump. Ian had slammed into platform 8, his body found at 3.40 a.m. by a security guard on a routine patrol. Martha looked along. At the north end of the bridge, the drop wasn't enough onto the metal roof of the covered platforms. At the south end, the raised curve of Market Street underneath reduced the falling distance by half. So this little gap here, uncovered platform 8, was by far the biggest fall you could manage. Just to be sure you didn't survive. How very considerate of him.

Martha hopped down. 'Come on.'

They turned at Drummond Street, past the sex shop and the old barber's, to number 42.

9

Cal shook his head. 'I haven't been here since that time we visited drunk. How old were we?'

'Thirteen. Same year as the diagnosis.' Martha did the 'mental' finger loop at the side of her head and crossed her eyes. Cal laughed.

Martha had been here since then, but not regularly. Ian was always crying off, too busy with work or other, vague stuff, just seemingly never the right time.

She raised a boot and kicked at the stairwell door. It was after two in the morning.

'Hey,' Cal said.

'I want to go in.'

Cal pulled her aside. 'Kicking down doors is man's work.'

He mugged being macho, showing off his muscles, then stepped back and placed a perfect heavy shoulder on the lock, which snapped open. That was another way they were different, Cal went to the gym most days, studied Taekwondo and played rugby. The nearest she got to a workout was lifting a pint to her lips.

They busted the flat door just as easily and went in. The place was a tip. A bachelor pad for a man in his forties with nothing to show for life. Carry-out food cartons and beer cans. A PS3. Some mood-stabilising medication in the bathroom cabinet, the seal unbroken.

On a low shelf Martha found the Walkman and the cassettes. Dozens of them, all with his scratchy handwriting. He had a tape deck on his hi-fi, so she slipped one in as Cal found a bottle of vodka in a cupboard and poured some into mugs. She looked at the cassette box. *Ten* by Pearl Jam.

Cal handed her a drink. 'So, this giving you the closure you need?'

Martha clinked mugs. 'Fuck off.'

'My poor, troubled sister.'

'I said, fuck off.'

They staggered out at five, the sun smudging the edges of rooftops, Martha with the Walkman and a handful of cassettes in her bag. Flagged a cab home to bed.

Now she was headed the other way. The bus was on London Road, then past the Playhouse and up Leith Street. Her stomach tightened as they turned onto North Bridge. She looked west. Stared at the castle, then the Standard Hotel, converted from the old newspaper offices. That must've been where Ian began working for the paper. In a time before her, before Cal, before the internet and smartphones and apps. When news was printed on paper. As foreign to her as the Stone Age.

She pressed the button and got off at the end of North Bridge. She pulled her coat tight and headed along the Royal Mile, past the tat shops and tourist trail, then down St Mary's Street to Holyrood Road. The Lemonheads finished doing a cover of that Paul Simon song from an ancient movie she'd seen with Cal, then the tape went silent. She pressed Stop and bundled the Walkman into her bag.

She was standing opposite the *Standard's* office, the Crags looming behind. The sun was high in the sky, hazy behind thin cloud. The wind was fresh, rustling the leaves on the trees in front of the building. Spring had arrived. She checked her watch. Five to midday. Five minutes early. She took a big breath, widened her eyes, tried to shake the past and the darkness from her brain, and crossed the road to her new job.

CHAPTER 3

'I'm here for work experience at the *Standard*, on the news desk. I'm supposed to report to the news editor.'

The receptionist was the same age as Martha, peroxide hair extensions, push-up bra too tight and sticky lip-gloss. 'Name?'

'Martha Fluke.'

'Fluke?'

'Yeah.'

'Take a seat.'

She stalked around the reception area trying to look casual, trying to feel calm, trying to breathe. Not long ago, the news editor would've been Ian. She didn't know if they'd replaced him yet. The plan had been that neither of them would reveal she was his daughter, didn't want accusations of cronyism or nepotism, even though he'd never really been much of a part of her life. The different surnames helped. She would be treated like any other third-year journalism student on Easter placement, exploited as free labour for three weeks, doing all the shittiest jobs. Now, with Ian's suicide, she was doubly sure about not revealing the connection. The last thing she wanted was to be connected to that stigma.

She pulled a small mirror out her bag and checked her makeup. Infinitely better than Little Miss Trowel-Face behind reception. Just a thin layer of natural lippy, a little smoky eye shadow and mascara to offset the blue eyes and auburn hair. Her eyes were her best feature, easy. Lips not bad either, a natural pout. Couldn't do anything about the stubby nose or the square jaw, but the spread of freckles across her cheeks helped a little. She tucked her hair behind one ear and put the mirror away.

'Fluke?'

Martha turned. A woman was swishing her pass on the security gate and waving her over. She was late twenties, black hair in a ponytail, and wore a Motörhead T-shirt with the cleavage and sleeves cut out. She had big tits, bigger biceps, a black eye and a cut lip.

Martha walked over and held out a hand. 'Martha.'

She got a slap on the back.

'I'm gonna call you Fluke cos it's a cool name.' The accent was American, somewhere Southern. 'I'm V.'

'V?'

'For Virginia. My asshole parents are eternally disappointed in my lack of virginal status.'

Martha stayed quiet.

V pointed at her eye. 'You're wondering about the shiner, right? You should see the other bitch.

14

I'm an amateur wrestler, helps let off steam after this stinking shitheap. Sorry, you're probably full of journalistic principles, right? Forget I said what a backstreet abortion of a paper this is.' V threw out a massive smile and nudged Martha's back. 'Come on, let's walk and talk.'

They headed for the stairs, V striding off, Martha scuttling behind.

'There's been a change of plan,' V said. 'You won't be working the news beat, at least not today.'

V took the stairs two at a time, Martha struggling to keep up.

'Why?'

V shrugged. 'Just the usual Monday shitstorm.'

'But I'm supposed to be doing news, that's what I'm studying.'

They were a flight up already, V holding the door open. They emerged into an open-plan office, thirty or so cheap desks, only half with computers and phones. Martha did a quick head count. Seven people.

'Where is everyone?'

V laughed. 'This is it.'

'What?'

'Welcome to the *Mary Celeste* of newspapers. Lay-offs and cost cutting. Don't get me started. Only reason you're here is cos they don't have to pay you. If they could run the whole paper with work experience lackeys they would.'

V was off again, heading to the darkest corner of the office, away from the large glass window at the front of the building where a couple of well buffed thirty-somethings were sitting gossiping.

'Don't even look at them,' V said, 'or you'll turn to stone. Or is it a pillar of salt?'

V was almost in the corner, two desks obviously in use surrounded by three empty ones.

'This is our exclusion zone,' V said. 'From the assholes.'

Martha looked at the desks. One covered in empty cartons of protein shakes, a pile of letters, pictures of male wrestlers pinned up everywhere, a sea of oiled muscle. The other desk was plain, just an in-tray with a couple of inches of paperwork in it.

'Pastyface didn't make it in today, *quelle surprise*,' V said. 'Chances are it's another stretch of long-term stress. Guy's got a doc in his pocket for sure. But this could work out well for you, one person's whatever-it-is being another one's whatchama-callit, if you get me.' She waved a hand vaguely. 'Over at the news desk you would get fuck-all writing done. They never give the Oompa-Loompas a break. With us, you'll be in print most days. Probably the whole time you're here, if Pastyface is true to form.'

'So what am I going to be doing?'

'Welcome to the dead beat.'

'What?'

V pulled out the chair at the desk. 'Congratulations Martha Fluke, you are the *Standard's* new obituary writer.'

CHAPTER 4

V edited the letters page. 'As well as doing a million and one other things around here.' She sucked on a protein shake. 'It's basically a magnet for psychos. The same little gang of self-important mentalists send me ridiculous emails every day, usually about wind farms or independence. Sometimes just to mix things up they'll write me an actual letter in green pen. They get filed straight in the bin.' She threw the empty shake carton onto her desk. 'Actually, the worst thing is that I have to read 'em all, you know, just in case Tony Blair or the Dalai fucking Lama sends in a vital missive and I accidentally use it to wipe my ass.'

She spent the next twenty minutes showing Martha the ropes of the dead beat. Martha was actually sitting in for the editor of the page, and the job was mainly commissioning out work to a handful of reliable freelancers, making sure she got stuff in, subbing it, setting it out on the page, also checking the other papers first thing to see if they'd missed any obvious deaths. But she would have to write shorter obits too.

Part of the job was manning the phones, dealing with the bereaved, giving them a sympathetic ear to talk to. They could get a bit crazy sometimes. Never get into an argument, and never admit responsibility for an error; the paper could get sued.

'We have to get the pages to bed by end of shift at eight p.m. It's usually pretty relaxed, but sometimes there's an almighty fuck-up and you have to work on.'

V showed her how the computer network was set up, pointed her at the appropriate folders. There was a folder full of advance obits of famous people ready to go. Prince Philip, Bruce Forsyth, all that.

'One other thing,' V said. 'If you get some widow or son on the phone, weeping away about their dearly beloved, try to get them to write something themselves.'

'Why?'

'If we get a family member or close friend to write something, it's called an appreciation rather than an obituary, and we don't need to pay 'em.'

'Is the paper really that strapped for cash?'

'You have no idea, honey-child.' V waved a hand around the office. There were even fewer people than were there earlier. 'All this will be dust in five years, believe me.'

Martha shook her head. 'Glad I'm getting into journalism, then.'

V laughed. 'That's the spirit.' She sprang out of

18

her seat and ripped one of the wrestling posters off her pinboard. 'Now, I'm off to the ladies for a quick wank.'

Martha raised an eyebrow and V looked at her watch. 'Only joking, it's a bit early for that nonsense. But I do need a massive shit. All these protein shakes.' She flexed her arms, kissed her biceps. 'Worth it, though, huh?'

She strode away with the poster clutched in her hand. She turned and walked backwards for a moment. 'While I'm gone, just read some obits, get a feel for them, and pray you don't get any crazies on the phone.'

CHAPTER 5

The phone on her desk rang.

She looked round. V was still gone. The two buffed floozies were still chatting half a mile away across the office. A dishevelled, lanky guy had slouched down at a desk closer to her, and was clicking a mouse.

She stared at the phone. Fumbled a notepad and pen out of her bag. Picked up the phone on the seventh ring.

'Hello, the obituary desk.'

'Who is this?' A man, middle-aged. He sounded very stressed.

'My name is Martha Fluke, I'm the obituary writer at the *Standard*.'

A pause. 'No you're not.'

'What?'

Silence. The man began sniffling, seemed on the edge of tears. One of the crazies V had warned her about, maybe. 'I have an obituary for you.'

'I'm sorry, your name is?'

A pause. 'I can't give you my name.' He was really crying now.

'That's not how things work, Mr . . .'

'I know how things work.' He was struggling to get the words out between gasps and sobs.

'You can email an appreciation to us.'

'Just write this down.'

There was panic in his voice, Martha could sense it down the line. She thought about her shorthand, forty-eight per cent in the last test. She spotted a jack dangling out from the phone handset.

'Just a minute.'

She dropped the handset and pulled the Walkman out her bag. Pushed a random cassette into it and plugged it into the phone. Backup. She pressed Record and Play, then picked the handset up again.

'Go ahead.'

'Gordon Harris died this week in tragic circumstances at his home, aged forty-five.'

Martha scribbled shorthand and watched the tape creep round the Walkman's spindle, hoping it was recording.

'He was educated at Inverness Academy, then the University of Edinburgh, after which he got a job on the *Standard* newspaper.'

'Wait . . .'

'He wasted the next twenty years of his life, cynical and jaded about everything he wrote, guilty and depressed because of everything he'd done in the past.'

'I'm sorry, this is inappropriate, it's not the kind of thing we print.'

'Please don't interrupt.'

Something in his voice kept Martha quiet. She

thought she heard a noise down the line between the sobs, the rustling of paper maybe, or the scrape of a hand on stubble.

'Gordon Harris was a terrible human being.' He was crying hard now, hardly able to speak.

Martha didn't say anything. Just let the crazies vent it all out, V had told her. Don't interrupt.

'He never did a good thing for anyone in his entire life, and he deserved to be haunted by guilt and depression. The manner of his death was a fitting end to his pathetic existence.'

He broke down into uncontrollable tears.

'Harris is survived by his wife Samantha and his mother Morag. He was born on the ninth of March 1969 and died on the thirty-first of March 2014.'

'That's today,' Martha said.

He could hardly speak through the sobs. 'I'm Gordon Harris.'

There was a loud bang.

Martha jumped and dropped the phone.

'Fuck.'

She picked it up again.

'Hello?'

Silence down the line.

'Hello? Mr Harris? Jesus Christ. What did you do? Gordon?'

Silence. Martha's heart was clattering. She tried to listen to the phone. Couldn't hear anything.

'Mr Harris, are you there?'

Was this a hoax, a prank they played on the new

girl in the office? Something in the guy's voice told her it wasn't.

She looked round the office. Only the slacker guy, sucking on a pen with his feet up on the desk. He had a thick pink scar across the back of his head.

'Hey you,' she shouted.

He swivelled round and raised his eyebrows at her.

'Do you know Gordon Harris?'

'Sure, he's the obit writer.'

'What?'

'That's his desk you're sitting at.'

She still had the phone handset in the crook of her neck. She waved it at him. 'I think he just shot himself while on the phone to me.'

'Shit.' The guy came over, limping a little. Held his hand out. Martha handed him the phone.

'Hello?' he said.

'He read me his own obituary, he was crying, then there was a sound like a gunshot.'

The guy's eyes widened. 'Oh shit, Pastyface has gone and done it. Did he say where he was?'

She consulted her shorthand. 'At home.'

The guy handed the phone back to Martha, who put it to her ear. Nothing. The guy lifted V's phone and pressed some buttons.

'Debbie, it's Billy Blackmore here. What's Gordon Harris's address?' A pause. 'I know you're not supposed to, but this is an emergency.'

A long beat.

'Christ's sake, Debbie, I won't say where I got it, just tell me.'

He scribbled something down on Martha's notepad.

'Thanks, Debs.'

He turned to Martha. 'Come on.'

'What?'

Billy looked at her. 'Let try to save this poor fucker's life.'

CHAPTER 6

They got a taxi from the rank outside the office. Billy held the door open for her, then ducked in and spoke to the driver. 'Twelve Noble Place, please, Leith Links.' He shut the door behind him. 'Listen, there might be someone dying there, so we need to get a shift on.'

The driver was young, Hibs tattoos and a crew cut. 'Shouldn't you call an ambulance?'

Billy waved his phone. 'I'm on it.'

The taxi did a U-turn and sped round the corner, past Holyrood Palace and the Parliament. Billy was on the phone, trying to explain, not getting very far.

They headed up Abbeyhill. Sat at the lights next to the Regent.

'I'm not running a red,' the driver said. 'We'd need that ambulance ourselves.'

Billy hung up. 'They're not coming.'

'Why not?' Martha said.

'Not until they know there's a definite incident. They think it could be a hoax.'

Martha stared at Billy. 'But you don't?'

Billy shook his head. 'I know Harris. This isn't a joke.'

They were pushed back into their seats as the taxi lurched forward at the lights.

Martha stuck out her hand. 'I'm Martha, by the way.'

Billy looked at her hand then shook it. 'Billy.'

He smiled. He had a squint smile, a red mark above his left eye. Martha thought about the scar at the back of his head, his limp. She smiled back.

'This your first day on the job?' he said.

'Yeah.'

'Welcome to the *Standard*, where every day's a big adventure.'

He laughed, but it faded as he furrowed his brow and stared down Easter Road.

Martha prayed this whole thing was a stupid, puerile joke.

They swung away from Leith Links into the colonies. Stopped at the end of Noble Place. There was no point trying to get the taxi down there, cars were double-parked all the way along.

Billy threw a tenner at the driver and opened the door. Loped up the street, Martha beside him, counting the houses.

Number 12 was the same as all the rest, modest grey stone, small bay windows, terraced normality.

Martha walked up the path and tried the door. Locked. She rang the doorbell as Billy banged on the door.

'Gordon?' he shouted. 'You in there?'

Martha went to the window, raised her hand to the glass to shield it from sunlight and peered in. She could see someone lying on a sofa, but couldn't make out the details.

'Someone's in there.'

Billy shouted through the letterbox. 'Gordon. Open the door. It's Billy from the office.'

They waited a few moments. Nothing.

Billy sized up the front door. Solid. He pushed his shoulder hard against it and grimaced. Rubbed at the back of his head.

Martha eased him out the way.

'Breaking down doors is women's work.' She raised a foot and kicked at the lock. The door shuddered. She kicked again.

Billy was at the window, squinting in. 'I think that's him. Can't see properly.'

Martha kicked a third time and the lock splintered away from the door jamb. She weighed a shoulder into it and it sprang open, then she was inside and through to the living room, Billy right behind.

'Jesus,' Martha said.

He was slumped sideways on the sofa, his legs still pointing forwards, as if he'd just been blown over by a breeze. Part of his face was missing and there was a gun slack in his left hand. Next to his right hand was the phone.

Martha took that hand and held his wrist, keeping her eyes away from the mess of his face.

Felt for a pulse. All she could hear was her own heartbeat flooding through her body. Tried to relax. She thought she felt something, yeah, definitely, a weak pulse, erratic, but holding on.

'He's still alive.'

Billy was on his phone.

'We need an ambulance, someone's shot himself.' Billy pulled a hand down over his face and made a 'please hold' face. 'Fucking hell,' he said to himself, then down the phone: 'Yeah, twelve Noble Place. Gordon Harris has tried to kill himself. Shot himself in the mouth, by the look of it.'

Martha glanced at Gordon and winced. His nose was gone, along with one eye, replaced by a mush of flesh and cartilage. There was a hole at the top of his head just at his hairline, ragged with blood, brains and bone. Behind his head, the sofa was dark and glistening. Blood was spattered up the wall behind, where he must've been sitting when he fired. Martha let go of his wrist and got up.

Billy ended the call. 'On their way. They'll be here as soon as they can.'

Martha breathed deeply. 'Are we supposed to do anything?'

Billy shook his head. 'Just wait.'

'We need to do something. We can't leave him like this.'

'We shouldn't move him.'

Martha stole a look at Gordon. His remaining eye was closed. If you ignored the mess of the rest of his face, he looked peaceful, could've been fast asleep.

28

'I can't look.' She turned to Billy, away from Gordon.

Billy put his hand on her back. 'It's OK.'

She looked at the phone handset. Fifteen minutes ago she was sitting in the office, listening to the sound of his voice. An hour before that she had been standing outside the *Standard* office, a future career as a news reporter ahead of her. An hour before that she was in a graveyard talking to her dead dad. She wanted to rewind her day back to that point, put a different tape in and press Play.

She knelt down at the handset.

'Don't touch it,' Billy said.

She looked at him.

'Potential crime scene.'

'Is attempted suicide a crime?'

Billy shrugged.

Martha knelt down and moved her head towards the phone, placing her ear as near as she could to the earpiece. She listened. Was it still connected to her line at the desk?

'Hello?' she said.

'What are you doing?'

'Shhh.' She waited. Nothing.

She remembered the Walkman. She hadn't pressed Stop. It would still be recording.

She adjusted her weight to move closer. Put her hand in a wet patch of carpet by Gordon's foot. Lifted her hand to her nose. Piss. She looked and saw a stain all down the front of his trousers.

She got up, holding her wet hand away from her like a radio-active spider.

'I need to find some soap,' she said.

'Maybe we should wait outside for the ambulance.'

It seemed obscene to leave him lying there, but what else could they do? He was unconscious, dying. But they weren't qualified and had been told not to touch him.

Martha found a bathroom and washed her hands. The decor was flowery, old-fashioned, a middle-aged woman's touch. She remembered. 'Harris is survived by his wife Samantha and mother Morag.'

Shit. Someone would have to break the news to them.

And Mrs Harris would have to clean up this mess. She would have to throw the sofa out, surely? Blood soaked in, blood up the walls, piss all over the carpet. Never mind the selfishness of leaving loved ones behind, what about the selfishness of leaving a mess of body fluids behind? Leaving parts of your face splattered up a wall, hidden down the back of the sofa, stuck to the skirting boards.

She went outside and joined Billy, who was sitting on the front step, scratching at the mark above his eye.

'This is fucked up,' Billy said.

Martha didn't say anything.

CHAPTER 7

She was jostled as the ambulance went over a speed bump. Gordon's body rocked. The paramedic placed a hand on his chest to steady him. He glanced at a heart-rate monitor then back at the body.

Gordon was strapped onto a stretcher. He had a gauze sheet over his face with a hole cut in it where the oxygen mask was. As well as the heart monitor and the oxygen, he was connected to an IV through a needle in his hand.

'How is he?' Martha said.

The paramedic shook his head. 'Not good.'

'What does that mean? Is he going to die?'

'Not if we can help it.'

The ambulance had the siren on and was racing south to the ERI. Speed bumps, red lights and traffic jams were everywhere, though.

Journalistic clichés ran through Martha's head. 'Race against time', 'dramatic shooting incident', 'matter of life and death'. None of them seemed to have any connection to the visceral brutality of Gordon's face, to the matter-of-fact nature of the violence it was possible to do to your own body.

And those clichés didn't convey any of the mundanity of her experience either. Martha and Billy had spent five minutes sitting outside the house before the paramedics turned up, as if they were just relaxing and soaking up the spring sunshine. They'd watched as the crew went about their business methodically, checking Gordon's injuries, administering medication, stabilising him. Talking on their radios to someone at the hospital throughout, medical jargon and lingo.

Martha turned to Billy now in the back of the ambulance and nodded towards Gordon.

'What's he like?' she said. She was aware as she spoke that she'd almost used the past tense. What was he like. Not dead yet. Hold on, you idiot.

'How do you mean?' Billy said.

'Just that – what's he like? As a person?'

Billy looked at the body laid out. 'Depressed? Suicidal?'

Martha raised her eyebrows.

'Sorry,' he said. 'I don't know him that well really. Keeps himself to himself. He's been the obit writer at the *Standard* as long as anyone can remember, I think. Takes a weird kind of mindset to do that job for so long. Surrounded by death every day. He's off sick with stress a lot. I guess he's not a happy bunny.'

'What's his wife like?'

Billy stared at her. 'He's married?'

'Jesus, didn't you ever talk to him?

'Yeah, but just small talk. He never mentioned

a wife. I presumed he was single. Are you sure he's married?'

'She's called Samantha. He told me on the phone.'

Billy shook his head. 'I wouldn't want to break the news to her.'

'Will the police do that?'

Billy shrugged. 'I guess so.'

The paramedic looked up. 'The police have been informed. They'll want to speak to you both at the hospital. Standard procedure.'

'Do you see a lot of this kind of thing?' Martha said.

He shook his head. 'Hardly ever gunshot wounds. There aren't many guns in circulation in this city.'

'What about attempted suicides?'

'Plenty of them. Pills or wrists usually. They're easy to deal with, the old "cry for help". Pump the stomach, stop the bleeding, fine. Hardly anyone dies that way.'

'What about guns?'

'Fewer people survive,' the paramedic said. 'But the best way to kill yourself is to jump off a high building or bridge.' He looked apologetic. 'Sorry, I don't mean "best", I mean "most effective".'

Martha tensed up. 'There was a jumper two weeks ago, off North Bridge. Did you deal with it?'

He shook his head. 'Wasn't my shift. I heard about it, though. They didn't need an ambulance, dead on impact.'

Billy looked at her. 'What's the interest in suicide? A hobby of yours?'

Martha's eyes felt suddenly heavy. 'Just wondering.'

She turned to him as they thudded over another speed bump. 'So what's your story?'

Billy's hand came up to the back of his head. 'You don't want to know.'

'Why did I ask, then? Come on, what do you do at the *Standard*?'

'I'm at the *Evening Standard*, actually. And I do the most boring job on the whole paper.'

Martha raised her hands. 'Don't leave me dangling with that juicy nugget. Something worse than obit writer?'

'Much worse. At least Gordon gets to write. I just lay out the Family Announcements page, you know, births, deaths and marriages. Except, actually, it's ninety-nine per cent deaths.'

'So you're on the dead beat too?'

'Yeah, but I don't get to write anything. The death announcements are all the same. All old folks, either going "peacefully" or "suddenly". No one ever rages against the dying of the light.'

'Doesn't sound like much of a job.'

'I also sub the puzzle page and . . .'

'What?'

Billy made a face. 'Write the horoscopes.'

'Really?'

'Don't laugh.'

'I thought that was some gypsy woman?'

Billy smiled and pointed at himself. 'Cut and paste.'

'But isn't there like a hotline or something?'

'That's just some woman with an accent reading it out. At least I don't have to do that.'

Martha sized him up. He was a few years older than her, mid-twenties, and there was a tiredness about his eyes, like he'd seen more of the world than he wanted to, than any twenty-five-year-old should. He was cute, though. Pretty, even. She thought about the scars, the limp, the sadness in his face. It was so like her, to fancy a hopeless case. Drawn to the damage. Didn't take Freud to work that shit out.

'How did you manage to land such an illustrious position?' she said. It came out more sarcastic than she meant, and she felt bad.

He laughed. 'I wasn't always such a high-flyer, you know, I used to . . .'

'What?'

His head was down. 'I'll tell you another time.' He looked up and held her eye. 'When I get to know you better.'

The paramedic stood up. 'If you two lovebirds are quite finished, we're here.'

CHAPTER 8

Martha and Billy hung around while he went into surgery, unsure what to do with themselves. Medical staff didn't know how long they'd be working on him.

'Depends on the mess we find in there,' a Dr Khan said.

They waited outside the double doors that led to surgery, flicking through magazines, shuffling on cheap fabric chairs in a small waiting alcove. Billy disappeared to track down some coffees, promising that he would call the office to let them know what had happened and why they weren't at their desks. Martha tried to imagine V's face when she heard. She wondered if the Walkman was still recording, or if it had run out of tape. She wondered which of her dad's albums she'd taped over with Gordon's obit. She realised that she didn't have her bag with her, had left it at the desk in the office. It already seemed like weeks ago that she'd sat down there and begun reading obituaries.

A woman came bustling down the corridor towards the nurse at reception. She was dowdy and dumpy, mousy hair in a ponytail, frayed business suit. She had a frantic look.

'Where's my husband?' she said.

The nurse was calm, used to all sorts of craziness here. 'Who is your husband?'

'Gordon Harris. The police called to say there had been an incident, that he was in hospital. I asked at A & E, they said to come here. Where is he, can I see him?'

The nurse scanned a computer screen, clicked the mouse. She was early twenties, false lashes, cerise nails clacking on the keyboard.

'Your husband is in surgery at the moment, Mrs Harris.'

'Surgery? What happened?'

The nurse pointed at the computer screen. 'That's all I have. If you take a seat, I'll go and see what I can find out through in the surgery unit.'

Samantha Harris was fidgeting, fingers thrumming on her handbag. 'Can't I come with you?'

A shake of the head. 'Restricted.'

The nurse came out from behind the reception desk. Her uniform had been taken in at the waist and the hem was shortened. More than halfway to tarty, a perv's wet dream. She swiped a security card at the lock and disappeared.

Martha got up and walked towards Samantha. She wasn't sure why, didn't know what she was going to say, but something compelled her to move her feet all the same.

'Mrs Harris?'

The woman turned. Confusion in her eyes. 'Yes? Who are you?'

'My name's Martha Fluke.'

'I don't know you.'

'No, I'm on work experience at the *Standard*.'

'Gordon hasn't mentioned you.'

'I just started today. I was covering for him because he was off sick.'

'He wasn't sick, why do you say that? I don't understand why you're here. What happened to Gordon?'

Martha felt a gravitational pull towards the other woman, an irresistible attraction. The police obviously hadn't told her.

'Maybe we'd better sit down,' she said. She tried to take Samantha's elbow, but the other woman pulled away.

'I don't want to sit down. Why would I need to sit down?'

'Samantha . . .'

'Don't use my name. I don't know you.'

Martha tilted her head towards the scratchy seats. 'I really think it's better if we take a seat.'

'Are you sleeping with Gordon?'

'What?'

A newfound aggression in the woman's voice. 'Is that what this is about?'

'Why would I . . . never mind. No, I'm not sleeping with anyone.' More than she meant to say.

Samantha's eyes narrowed. 'Just tell me what you know.'

Martha looked round, hoping Billy or the police or the nurse would come and save her from this. But there was no one.

'Gordon phoned the obituary desk this morning.'

'To phone in sick, yes?'

'No,' Martha said. 'He began dictating an obituary. He seemed distressed. The obituary was his own. Then he shot himself while still on the phone.'

'What?'

'He shot himself.'

'With what?'

'Pardon?'

'With what?'

'A gun.'

'Don't be stupid, Gordon doesn't have a gun.'

Silence for a moment.

'Why?' Samantha said.

'I'm sorry?'

'Why would he do something like that?'

Martha looked at her and felt a wave of empathy rush over her. 'He tried to kill himself, Mrs Harris. He attempted suicide.'

The light went out of Samantha's eyes. A heavy realisation and understanding.

'Shit,' she said.

'I'm sorry.'

'Shit.' Her legs gave way beneath her. Martha caught her arm as she slumped, but didn't have enough strength to hold her up. Instead Samantha's weight dragged them both down to a clumsy thump on the floor. They sat on the ground, thin blue carpet under their backsides, Samantha with tears in her eyes.

'How did you find him?'

'What?'

'If he was on the phone, how did you find him?'

'My colleague got his address from HR, we jumped in a taxi and broke the door in.'

Samantha shook her head. 'You broke down our front door?'

'Yes.'

'How did he have a gun?'

'What?'

'Gordon doesn't own a gun.'

It was Martha's turn to shake her head. 'I don't know.'

'How is he?'

'I don't know that either. We came with him in the ambulance, but they took him straight through there.' Martha nodded towards the double doors.

It felt weird, sitting on the floor, like being back at primary school. Martha could see a piece of chewing gum stuck under the reception desk, a few dust bunnies in the corner of the room. The ceiling seemed impossibly far away.

Samantha was sobbing, wiping her eyes with her sleeve.

'Maybe we should get up,' Martha said.

Their legs were kind of tangled together. Samantha leaned in to Martha and laid her head on her shoulder. Martha thought about snot and tears. Then thought about her dad jumping from North Bridge, the 'most effective' way to go. Don't ever shoot yourself in the face, kids. She wondered if the surgeons would keep Gordon Harris alive, and what kind of existence he would have if they did, with half his face missing. What would Samantha think of that?

'Mrs Harris?'

Martha looked up. A male and a female police officer were towering over them.

CHAPTER 9

'Explain it to me again.'

Martha explained it again.

The police had split them up. Samantha was in one corner of the waiting room with the female cop, hunched over on a seat with a tissue pressed to her nose, the policewoman in close, communing with her. Martha had got the male cop, who was being a lot less cosy. She tried to imagine what it would be like to be married to someone and have them blow half their face all over your living-room sofa and walls. The female cop reached out and touched Samantha's knee. Martha thought about the male cop touching her leg. He was tall and dark but not handsome, an outsized human in his anti-stab vest, clumpy boots, and with all the familiar cop paraphernalia hanging from his belt like he was Batman.

As she told the officer again what had happened, she left out the part about recording the phone conversation.

'Then what happened?' The cop had a notebook and pencil out. Very old school. Didn't they have iPads now? She wondered if they got taught during training a certain way to take police notes, like she studied shorthand.

She explained about Gordon crying down the phone, revealing who he was, then the sound of a gun. She explained about Billy getting the address and the two of them going round.

'And where is this Billy Blackmore?' the cop said.

She looked around. Good question.

'He went to get coffee.'

But that was ages ago. Maybe he left the hospital, left her to deal with all this herself. Lovely.

She described what they'd found in Noble Place, screwing up her face at the gory details. He jotted it all down diligently. She gave her number and address, in case they needed to contact her again.

'Why would you need to get in touch again?' Martha said.

'We won't, it's just standard procedure. But this seems a simple attempted suicide. The only interesting thing is where he got a gun.'

The only interesting thing. Something occurred to Martha.

'Where is the gun?'

She couldn't remember seeing it after the paramedics arrived.

The cop's radio crackled.

'There are other officers at the scene,' he said. 'And forensics. They'll take care of that.'

'You got the grieving widow shift, yeah?'

The cop frowned. 'She's not a widow, miss. At least, not yet.'

'Sorry.'

Why did she let her mouth run away with her sometimes?

The double doors to surgery opened and the slutty nurse came through with Dr Khan from earlier. Samantha bolted out of her chair, shredded tissue clutched in her hands. Martha got up too and walked over, she wanted to hear this.

'Mrs Harris?' Khan said. He was tiny, the shortest person in the room, with delicate bones and a high voice.

She nodded and sniffed.

'Your husband is alive, but in a coma,' he said. 'His condition is very serious, I'm afraid. We stabilised and cleaned up his wounds as best we could, but there has been significant trauma to the face and brain. He'll be taken to ICU and monitored. We won't know about his brain function or vital signs for a while. It's a waiting game now. I'm sorry it's not better news.'

'Can I see him?'

Dr Khan was already trying to extricate himself from her, his body language screaming that he had to be somewhere else.

'Of course, upstairs in intensive care.' He nodded to the nurse. 'Charlene can show you where that is.'

The nurse looked put out, turning a sarcastic smile at the surgeon, but she took Samantha by the arm anyway.

As soon as they were heading away, Dr Khan vanished back through the double doors. Martha's cop got a call on his radio and indicated to his partner that they were heading too.

'If we need anything else we'll be in touch,' he said as they clumped away.

She was alone in the waiting room.

Billy arrived round a corner with two coffees.

'Good timing, you just missed the cops.'

He looked sheepish. 'I know, I was waiting for them to leave.'

He handed a cup to her.

'Why?' she said.

'I just have a thing about cops.'

'That's not a good enough answer.'

'OK, cops have a thing about me.'

'That still isn't good enough.'

'Let's just say that I'm known to the police.'

'You have a record?'

'Not exactly.'

'Let me guess, armed robbery and murder?'

'I'll tell you later.'

She looked at him. 'You are such a fucking tease.'

Billy looked at the doors to surgery. 'What did the doc say?'

'Don't change the subject, we were talking about your previous encounters with Lothian and Borders' finest.'

'No, we weren't.'

Something in his voice made her drop it.

'Gordon is alive but in a coma. They don't know if he's going to come out of it.'

'And where did Nurse Tarty-pants take his wife?'

'Upstairs to intensive care.'

Billy took a sip of his coffee, thinking. Martha did likewise. It tasted of hot piss.

'Fancy a trip up to intensive care, then?' Billy waved his phone at her. 'I'm under instruction from the office to interview Samantha. Just in case it makes a story.'

'The paper would run a story on its own obit writer trying to kill himself?'

Billy shook his head and blew on his coffee. 'Not normally, but the gun is an interesting angle. Anything involving guns makes punters pick up the paper. We like to believe we're living in down-town Detroit.'

'That's a bit cynical.'

Billy made a goofy face. 'I thought you wanted to be a news reporter?'

'I do.'

'Then start acting like one and maybe we won't be stuck writing about dead people for the rest of our lives.'

CHAPTER 10

Billy crumpled his coffee cup into a bin and headed for the reception desk of the intensive care ward. Martha tagged along behind.

'Look upset and follow my lead,' Billy said.

He furrowed his brow and spoke to the nurse. This one was in her thirties, short hair, lip stud and Arabic tattoos.

'We're here to see our dad,' Billy said. 'I think he's just been brought up from surgery. Gordon Harris. Our mum should be here already.'

'She just went through,' the woman said. She was immediately mothering him. She checked her screen. 'He's in room six, I'll buzz you through.'

'Thank you.' Billy's voice was earnest, troubled.

The security door clicked and he pulled it open. So easy.

At the other side of the door, Billy shook his head. 'Security in this place is terrible.'

They found room six.

Gordon didn't look much different from earlier in the ambulance. Laid out on a bed, connected to various machines, bandages around his head, an oxygen mask over an opening at his mouth.

Samantha sat crying next to him, holding his limp hand. They stood watching her from the doorway. She let go of his hand, which fell to the bed. Then she slapped it.

'You idiot,' she said. 'I hate you for this.'

She slapped his hand again, twice.

Martha stage-coughed. Samantha turned slowly, unashamed.

'What are you doing here?'

'Just wanted to see how Gordon was doing,' Martha said.

She introduced Billy. She could see him switching on a small MP3 recorder in his pocket, the green light winking. He sat next to Samantha with the recorder nearest to her and put his hand on top of hers.

Billy spoke quietly to her and she replied in stops and starts, angry and confused and distressed. He comforted her. Martha watched them in a daze. This was what it meant to be a news reporter, secretly recording a conversation with a woman as she sat weeping next to her husband in a coma. Martha had spent three years studying the theories and skills of journalism, but never once pictured a scenario like this. Maybe she was just naïve. She felt a tremble in her stomach as Billy and Samantha whispered to each other.

She came round to the other side of the bed and stood next to the heart-rate monitor. She could smell antiseptic and that adhesive you get on plasters. Here was a man who had destroyed his own head trying to end it all, and he smelt like a kid with a grazed knee. She breathed deeply, wanted to get a scent of death or destruction into her lungs, but there was nothing. She closed her eyes. Pictured Gordon sitting up, casually unwrapping the bandages from his head. She realised she didn't even know what he looked like when he had all his face. All she could picture was the raw, bloody flesh where his nose should be, the empty eye socket, red and angry and accusing.

She opened her eyes.

Billy patted Samantha's hand and gave her a business card.

'If you need anything, Samantha, anything at all, just get in touch. Please. Gordon is a good friend.'

She nodded and sniffed as Billy got up, angling his head for them to leave.

CHAPTER 11

'Let's hear it, then.'

Martha was in McNeil's office, a large glass box at the back of the building overlooking the Crags. She didn't know his first name and no one had used 'Mister' when referring to him, just McNeil. He was in his fifties, white hair, broken nose. Solid, no bullshit. He was the editor of the *Standard*.

Also in the office were Billy and a woman Martha was introduced to as Rose, veteran crime reporter on the *Standard*. Rose was a handsome woman, maybe hitting fifty, curvy in a red blouse, matching heels and big gold hoop earrings. Martha liked her immediately.

She lifted the Walkman from her bag and McNeil raised his hand.

'Wait, what the hell is that?'

'A Sony Walkman.'

'What I meant to ask was what fucking decade is this? Have I slipped back in time and emerged in the early nineties?'

'It's all I have,' Martha said.

'Give it here,' McNeil said.

50

She handed it over. She had rewound the tape to the start of the side when she got back to her desk, or rather Gordon's desk. V had greeted her with wide eyes as she slumped in her seat, already up to speed thanks to a call from Billy.

'I covered for you,' V said. 'Christ on a bike, though. Pastyface, huh?'

Billy had come over a couple of minutes later. 'McNeil wants to see you.'

'McNeil?'

'Your boss.'

Martha looked at V.

V made a shooing motion with both hands, a theatrical gesture. 'Shit, girlfriend, go talk to McNeil. This could be a break. I don't really need a work experience here, I can do three jobs at once. I've been doing that for months anyhoo.'

Billy pointed at the Walkman on the desk. 'Bring that.'

McNeil was turning it round in his hands now. 'Shit the bed, it's heavy, eh?' He flipped the tape slot open then snapped it closed. Fiddled with the back, removed the battery cover then slid it back in. 'Is it at the start of the tape?'

Martha nodded.

McNeil pressed Play and they all listened.

The sound of her own voice was disconcerting, too high and squeaky. She was glad that she'd been polite. She listened to Gordon's voice. He was shitting himself, she could hear it.

As she listened, she was replaying the whole

51

conversation in her memory, already burned in there for ever. The others in the room were once removed from it, just voices on an old cassette, but she was right back there, at the desk, scribbling her crappy shorthand, gazing at the mess of V's desk, wondering when this nutter was going to get off the phone so she could relax.

But she couldn't relax. Then or now. She was tensing up in the office, aware of what was coming, the climax of it, the brutal snapping of this chain of words being casually spilled onto magnetic tape. Rearranging the ions. She was gripping the strap of her bag tightly, holding her breath, her jaw sore from clenching her teeth.

Bang.

She jumped all over again.

Everyone else in the room tensed as well. They were all uselessly staring at the Walkman sitting on McNeil's desk. The tape spools kept turning. Martha thought that was indecent – didn't they know what had just happened? Didn't they know it was over? They should stop out of respect.

'Shit,' McNeil said.

Rose and Billy shook their heads.

Martha heard her own voice swearing on the tape, shouting down the line. Then calling on Billy. This was Groundhog Day, living it over and over. It had only happened this morning and it was already a myth, cemented into her life. She tried to imagine telling this story twenty years from now around a middle-aged dinner party. She couldn't. Too personal, too private, she would be exposing too much of herself.

The four of them stood in silence, just the hiss of the cassette, a tiny creak of its old motor mechanism. McNeil reached forward and switched it off.

He turned to Rose. 'Well?'

She shook her head, still staring at the Walkman. 'Shit,' she said. 'Gordon. I can't believe it.'

'You knew him pretty well, right?' Billy said.

Rose looked at him. 'A long, long time ago. Haven't had anything to do with him recently.'

Something in her voice made Martha think that wasn't the whole truth.

'What do you think?' McNeil asked her. 'Any angle I'm missing?'

Rose frowned. 'It's not news. Except maybe the gun.'

'Yeah, that's what I figured,' McNeil said. 'You happy for Billy the Kid to keep tabs on it for now?'

Rose looked at Billy. There was something between the two of them. A closeness. A kindness, maybe.

'Yeah, that's fine.'

McNeil turned to Billy. 'OK, hotshot, keep in touch with the cops about the gun and let us know if you hear anything. But don't let it get in the way of your regular work with the evening paper.'

McNeil looked at his watch, a chunky silver thing. 'Balls, I have a meeting upstairs with some management in nappies. We're done here.' He turned to Martha. 'Thanks for bringing this to me.' Something seemed to occur to him. 'Are you all right? I mean, the shock and that.'

Martha nodded as she picked up the Walkman and put it back in her bag.

McNeil turned to Billy. 'This could be the start of your rehabilitation, Billy boy, don't fuck it up.'

He turned to Martha. 'And you're work experience, yeah?'

Martha nodded.

McNeil gave a dry smile. 'Well, it seems we need cover on the obit desk for a while.'

'I suppose,' Martha said.

'Keep in touch with Billy on this. You never know, could turn into something. And both of you report to Rose if you discover anything. Understand?'

They both nodded, like schoolkids being told off.

Martha glanced at Rose, who looked like she was somewhere else, frowning to herself.

'Now, all of you get out my office,' McNeil said. 'I have to go and explain to some quisling fucks how to run a newspaper.'

CHAPTER 12

Martha and Billy stood outside McNeil's office.

'What did he mean about your rehabilitation?' Martha said.

Billy looked at his watch. 'I'll tell you another time.'

Martha shook her head. 'International man of mystery, eh?'

Rose came out the office behind them.

'Billy, I'm just heading home, my shift's over. You need me to pick up anything on the way?'

'No thanks, I'm fine.'

'OK, see you back at the flat, then.'

Rose still looked like she was fretting over something. Martha watched her go. She had a great figure for someone kicking fifty. Martha turned to Billy.

'You live with her?'

'Not like that.'

Martha smiled, on the wind-up. 'Like what? I never said anything.'

'But I know what you were thinking.'

'She's a good-looking cougar right enough.'

'Stop it.'

'Into the MILF thing, yeah?'

'I said stop.' A serious tone in his voice, she'd touched a nerve. 'I'm sleeping in her spare room. Rose helped me out when I needed it. You have no idea. She's a good friend.'

'OK.'

'I only met you six hours ago and you've already got me into some crazy shit.'

'I already got us both a possible news story, you mean.'

Billy shook his head. 'Just go back to your desk and write some nice obituaries, OK?'

CHAPTER 13

So that's what Martha did.

Despite V's claims from earlier, deadline was approaching and they didn't have the pages properly laid out yet. Martha chased one of the freelancers and got copy in, then began subbing it onto the page. Standard eight-hundred-worder on some retired old colonel. It seemed like the vast majority of their obits were ex-army officers who'd seen out their last years shooting animals on Highland estates. Lots of pictures of old guys with whiskers standing next to mounted deer heads and the like. Martha wondered why they didn't do obits of ordinary people. It seemed like a last bastion of class snobbery – only the well-to-do were worthy of having their lives laid out for the ever dwindling readership to pore over as they sipped their morning tea or mid-afternoon Pimm's or whatever.

V got her letters pages finished early and helped out with the last scraps of stuff to do, all the fiddly stuff which seemed to take much longer than it should've. Then at 7.53 p.m. the pages were fixed and sent, and Martha and V leaned back in their chairs like old pros and made puffing noises.

'Some first day on the job, huh?' V said.

'Yeah.'

'That thing with Pastyface was fucked up.'

'Yeah.'

V reached into her desk drawer and pulled out a tartan Thermos flask, the kind that old grannies use. She unscrewed it and took a long, showy drink, then wiped her mouth and the rim of the flask and handed it over.

'Maker's Mark,' she said. 'Proper bourbon. None of that Jack Daniel's crap.'

Martha took the flask and looked round the office. It was busier now than earlier, but still only about half the desks were occupied. Billy was at his desk, tapping away.

'Drinking on the job?' Martha said to V.

She shrugged. 'Whatever gets you through the nightmare, missy.'

Martha took a slow pull from the flask and felt the heat rising in her. She passed the flask back.

'What's the deal with Billy over there?'

'The original gangster.'

'What does that mean?'

'You don't know?'

Martha shrugged.

'Don't you read the papers, Fluke?' V took a swig from the flask and handed it over. 'I thought you wanted to be a news reporter? I suppose this was a couple of years ago, you might've still been in short pants back then.'

Martha took a drink.

V leaned in. 'Well, it's not like me to gossip, but that's Billy Blackmore. Ring any bells?'

'Not really.'

'I'll give you a clue. Trainee crime reporter for the *Evening Standard*. Hit and run. Killed a crime lord. Got involved with the widow. Started a gangland feud.'

Martha's eyes widened. 'That was him?'

V smiled. 'Oh yeah. Our pretty little paper tried to play it down, but the tabloids went to town on him.'

'Shouldn't he be in prison?'

V tapped her nose. 'Prosecution fell through. Some misfiled paperwork, if you believe that bullshit. I think our Billy got very lucky or had friends in high places. Nobody gave a shit that a few drug dealers were dead. I think they were secretly happy that he'd done the city a public service.'

'And he's back working here?'

'More friends in high places. He's fucking that big tart Rose Brown on the crime desk.'

'He says he's not.'

'He would. And she knows McNeil really well, if you catch my drift. So they took him back on. Mind, they gave him the shittiest job in the whole building, and that includes the poor sap who has to clean the toilets after I've been in there. Penance, I guess.'

Martha stared at Billy as she took the flask from V. She sipped and burned. Thought about Billy and Rose, about car crashes and injuries.

V took the flask back and screwed the lid on.

'Speaking of the toilets, I'm away for a colossal dump then off to the gym. I need to be in tip-top shape for my next bout. It's tomorrow, you should come. Here.' She raked about in her drawer, pulled out a flyer and handed it over. 'Bring the original gangster, he looks like he could do with a night out. It could be your first date, how romantic.'

'Shut up,' Martha said as she folded the flyer into her pocket.

V pulled on her coat. 'You not leaving?'

Martha looked at Billy then back at V. 'I'll hang around for a bit.'

V sucked her teeth and made for the bogs.

'The girl likes a bad boy,' she said. 'Shit, I can relate.'

CHAPTER 14

Martha logged into the archive system using Gordon's account name and password, like V had shown her. It felt like he was already dead and she had replaced him. Fucked up.

Keyed in 'Billy Blackmore' and scanned the results.

Shit, what a story. She half-remembered it from the time. She looked at the dates on the articles. V was partly right, it was just before Martha had started ECT. She'd been in a black hole back then, the depression like a wet towel smothering her. There were whole periods of her life obscured, blanked from her mind, and that didn't include the short-term memory loss of ECT, just the terrible oblivion of the depression destroying everything that went along with it, every breath of air she took under its suffocating wings.

This thing with Billy was a mess. He was drinking and on drugs and hit a gangster, killed him. He'd reported on the story, got involved with the dead man's widow. Then there was a shoot-out up on the Crags that ended with two more guys dead and the whole cliff on fire. Jesus. She pressed Print on a handful of the stories, watched as the cheap printer on the desk spat the pages out.

Then she searched for 'Ian Lamb'. Hundreds of articles with his byline on them, of course. Nothing about his death that she could see.

She searched 'North Bridge' and got this from the *Evening Standard* on the day after he jumped:

Man Dies in Bridge Fall

Police have confirmed that a man has died after falling from North Bridge last night. The body of the man was discovered on platform 8 of Waverley Station at about 3.40 a.m.

There was no disruption to train services and no road closures.

Ambulance crews attended but the man was pronounced dead at the scene. There are no suspicious circumstances.

She highlighted the text on the screen and clicked Word Count. Sixty words. Sixty words to describe the life and death of her father, of someone who worked for this company for God knows how many years. Not much more than one word per year of his life. Pathetic.

She clicked Print.

The sheet that came out was mostly blank.

She searched 'Gordon Harris'. A whole raft of

obits with his byline on them. She scrolled down and stopped. There was Ian's obit. Why hadn't she thought of it before? Wait a minute, why hadn't she found it just before, when she searched his name? They'd used his full name, Ian Martin Lamb, and the search engine hadn't picked it up. That is some crap search engine.

She clicked through and began to read it on screen.

'Working late on your first day? You're keen.'

She jumped. Billy was standing across from her. Her eyes darted down to the desk. The reports on Billy's exploits were hidden underneath the North Bridge story. She scooped up all the papers and threw them into her bag.

'Just reading some obits,' she said. 'Getting a feel for it.'

'Fancy going for a drink?' Billy said. 'It's been quite a day. I thought maybe you could use one. I know I could.'

Martha looked at her screen. Billy couldn't see it from his side. The obit was accompanied by a picture of her dad she'd never seen before, a fuzzy black-and-white image of him holding a pint glass, surrounded by other drinkers, smiles on their faces. It was at least fifteen years old. He was grinning but there was something sad about his face too, a shadow across his brow that didn't seem to fit with the occasion.

There was so much she didn't know about him, so much she would never know.

'Hello?' Billy said. 'That drink?'

He peered over to look at her screen. She quickly clicked Print then closed the window before he could see. She grabbed her dad's obit as the printer chugged it out, then flipped it into her bag.

'Why not.'

CHAPTER 15

They were heading up the Royal Mile, all tartan and kilt shops. It was half eight but still light, spring trying to cast a cheery glow on the evening, but the strong westerly in their faces was putting paid to that idea. Tourists and drinkers tottered along on the cobbles around them.

'Where do you want to go?' Billy said.

'I said I'd go see my brother after work,' Martha said. 'Tell him how my first day went.'

'Think he's in for a bit of a shock.'

They were at the junction with the Bridges now. The Basement was down on Broughton Street. She knew what that meant.

She turned down North Bridge. 'This way.'

She didn't seem able to avoid the place. Or maybe she wasn't trying to. Maybe she was picking at the scab for all she was worth. Sounded about right.

They were walking down the east side of the bridge. She'd always preferred this side before Ian had ruined it for her. Everyone new to the city walked on the other side, pointing their cameras and phones at the castle and the Scott Monument, the stretch of Princes Street. But she preferred the view the other way, the beautiful calmness of the sea, the islands out there, the thin spread of Fife and East Lothian you could see on a clear day. Edinburgh was a beautiful bastard at times, whichever way you looked. But she could never look at this view the same way again.

She stopped at a sign. Bolted onto the stonework, low down:

> Samaritans.
> Who cares?
> We do.

Some joker had changed 'do' to 'don't' with a black marker. The phone number to call at the bottom was obscured by a ripped fly-poster for a Festival comedian from two years ago.

Billy was next to her, looking at the sign.

'You know they used to have a dedicated phone here,' he said. 'A hotline to the Samaritans. But they had to take it down because it kept getting vandalised. They figured it was better to have no phone than a broken phone. Sent out the wrong message.'

Martha stared at him. 'I think that's the saddest thing I've ever heard.'

She crouched down and touched the Samaritans sign. Because of the design of the wall it was about knee height, that was the only place it could fit amongst the crenellations. Which meant it was totally useless. She was surprised she'd noticed it; she hadn't before. She wondered if her dad had seen it, if the graffitied message had produced a smile on his face, the same sad smile in his obit picture.

Martha got up again and looked over Waverley Station, followed the lines of the track with her eyes.

'Is this something to do with earlier?' Billy said. 'In the ambulance you asked about a jumper.'

She kept her face turned away from him, towards the horizon, towards infinity.

'It was my dad.'

'Jesus Christ, I'm sorry. I suppose it's more common than you think. Someone from the office did the same a couple of weeks ago.'

She looked at him.

He understood. 'Wait, your dad is Ian Lamb?'

She pursed her lips together, made a slight movement of her head.

'Was.'

'Holy shit.'

'I didn't really know him,' Martha said. 'My mum and dad split before I was even born.'

'Still.' Billy rubbed the back of his head. 'He was a good guy, Ian. I mean, I didn't know him well, but nobody had a bad word to say about him in the office.'

'They're hardly going to go around slagging off the dead, are they?'

Martha rubbed the Samaritans sign, like a super-
stition, then turned.

She looped her arm through Billy's.

'Let's get drunk.'

CHAPTER 16

'So the guy I was covering for today phoned in his own obituary, then shot himself.'

'Ha, ha.'

'While still on the phone to me.'

'Stop it, please, my sides may split.'

'I'm not joking.'

Cal stared at her. 'You're not joking.'

Martha raised her hands like it was a stick-up. 'Honest, guv.'

'Shit the bed. Are you OK?'

Martha nodded. 'Two long vodkas, thank you, sibling.'

The Basement was empty. Monday night, after all, not exactly party central. Only Cal and an older woman working. The woman was mid-thirties, covered in tattoos and wore a bastardised Bratz T-shirt with 'Slutz' scrawled across it. Cal wore a tight grandad shirt over rippling muscles, his arse packed tight into red skinny-fit jeans.

Cal made a face. 'Fucking angostura bitters.'

He got on with the rigmarole of making the drinks.

'I know you only order these to annoy me,' he said. 'I'm sure you don't even like them.'

'I was born to annoy you, Cal.'

Cal emptied out the ice and bitters, filled the glass again. 'So, tell me about this guy on the phone.'

'This is Billy,' Martha said, waving a hand. 'He came to my rescue.'

'Not exactly,' Billy said, offering up a hand.

Cal looked at him. 'My hands are full making my sister's stupid drinks. But hi.'

He put the drinks on the bar in front of them and waved away Martha's attempt to pay. 'I've got free drinks in the till like you wouldn't believe.'

'We saved the guy's life,' Martha said. 'I think. He's in a coma anyway.'

Cal checked the bar – no waiting punters. He leaned forward and placed his chin on his hand.

'So, tell all, chicken.'

She did. The obit desk, the call, the shooting, the taxi, the hospital. In between she sooked her vodka through a straw and glanced at Billy. Felt like touching his damaged face. She'd read in one of those news reports that he'd had some kind of brain surgery, which explained the scarring at the back of his head. She wanted to feel what the skin was like, see if she could feel the tremor of damage underneath.

After delivering more long vodkas, Cal gave himself the night off since there were no punters to serve, and joined them at the drinking side of the bar. They moved on to Jägermeisters. Stupid, but Martha told herself she didn't have to start

70

till noon. How bad could the morning damage be? And she needed this, needed the release.

Martha turned to Cal. 'I told Billy about Ian. We walked from the office down North Bridge.'

'So you've seen the scene of the crime,' Cal said.

'Suicide's not a crime.'

'Isn't it?' Cal tilted his head. 'I don't know why you give a shit, sis. The prick left Mum as soon as he found out she was expecting us.'

'She kicked him out,' Martha said.

'You guys are twins?' Billy said. 'I didn't realise.'

Cal rolled his eyes and nudged Martha. 'He's about to say we don't look alike.'

'Everyone says that,' Martha said.

Billy smiled. 'Well, you don't.'

Martha kept her eyes on Billy's face as she downed her shot. She could get used to that smile.

CHAPTER 17

'I can't believe they haven't fixed the door yet,' Martha said. 'Don't these people want to be secure in their homes?'

She pushed the door open and headed upstairs to Ian's flat. Cal and Billy gave each other a look as they followed. The door to the flat was wedged closed, the lock still broken, but a small nudge opened it.

'This feels wrong,' Billy said. 'Breaking and entering.'

'We didn't break in,' Martha said. 'Well, we did last time, not this time.'

She turned to Cal. 'Billy is just a bit nervous about breaking the law. He's "known to police", as we journalists say.'

Cal put on a mock impressed face. 'Really?'

Martha tapped her nose and spoke in a stage whisper. 'It's a secret.'

In the living room, Martha headed for the alcove shelf with the spirits on it. She examined the bottles. 'He doesn't like to talk about it. But I heard a rumour down at the office.'

'V,' Billy said.

Cal looked puzzled. 'V?'

Martha held up a bottle of schnapps and squinted. 'This crazy American woman, into wrestling. You'd love her, Cal, she's nuts. It's V for Virginia.' She turned to the boys. 'Yes, V mentioned something, then I did a little research of my own, so you might as well come clean.'

'If you pour us some drinks I will,' Billy said, slumping into a sofa.

Martha disappeared to get glasses from the kitchen, then re-emerged clinking three in her hand. Poured out hefty measures and handed them out.

'I was involved in a hit and run,' Billy said to Cal. 'It was pretty complicated. I'd been drinking. The guy I hit was a criminal.'

'A crime lord, in journalistic parlance,' Martha said, waving her drink.

Cal's eyes lit up. 'Oh shit, you're that guy from the news a couple of years ago.'

'He's that guy,' Martha said, examining her dad's shelves of albums.

Billy raised his schnapps and sipped.

'Shouldn't you be in prison?' Cal said.

Martha pulled an album from the shelf. 'That's exactly what I said.'

Billy shrugged. 'I got lucky.'

Martha looked up from the album she was holding. It had a monkey with a halo on the front cover. 'I heard it was more than luck.'

Billy shook his head. 'You heard wrong, I was just lucky. The prosecution fucked up.'

Cal turned to Martha. 'You really pick 'em, don't you?'

'I haven't picked anyone,' Martha said. She held up the record. 'Either of you heard of The Pixies?'

She put the album on. Thudding bass, jagged guitars, some guy shouting about a debaser over the top, a girl talking in the background. Martha liked it, it was a bit unhinged. She started to sway to the rhythm, dancing with the album cover in one hand, her schnapps glass in the other.

'Weird to think of our dad being into this,' she said.

Cal frowned. 'He wasn't really our dad.'

Martha stopped dancing. 'Of course he was. If he wasn't, who the hell was?'

'No one.'

'Do you think Mum was into this music too?'

'Probably.'

Martha shook her head. 'I don't think I've ever heard her listen to music, have you?'

Cal shrugged.

Martha turned the volume up and went back to examining the shelves. Cal and Billy were talking, but she couldn't make out what about.

On one shelf low down she pulled out the box of cassettes she'd pilfered from last time. She flicked through. Bands she'd never heard of – Dinosaur Jr., Hüsker Dü, Mudhoney. A song called 'Touch Me I'm Sick' on that last one. She put it in her bag. She tried to imagine her dad when he was her age, listening to this stuff, full of righteous anger or miserably depressed or whatever. Couldn't get her head round it.

She kept rummaging through the box. There were tapes in here with just names on them, like people's names, with dates alongside. She realised they must be interview tapes for work. The dates were all over the place, some over ten years old, some from the last few months. She pulled one out and opened it. The insert card had been turned inside out, and it had track listings for albums by The Descendents and Dead Kennedys inside.

So he'd been taping over his musical past with boring work interviews. Erasing the songs that he'd once loved with chatter that paid the bills. She looked at the names of the interviewees, none of them meant anything. No famous politicians or whatever. He'd been a news reporter, then news editor, after all. You hardly interviewed anyone once you became an editor. That was one of the strange things about journalism she'd discovered on her Napier course – as soon as you got promoted to editor you were chasing other people's copy, telling them what to write, tracking down pictures, making sure it all went together properly. And you rarely got to write any more, presumably the thing you loved doing in the first place. Stupid.

She realised these interview tapes would have Ian's voice on them. She grabbed a handful and shoved them into her bag. She wanted to hear his voice.

She pulled the box out further and spotted something behind. A loose wooden panel at the back of the alcove had come away. She could see something behind it. She nudged it out the way and reached in. She pulled out a black A5 notebook. Opened it. Her dad's scrawl across the pages. It was dense, sloping, filled every page to the edges. There was a date on the first page, 22.7.91, two years before she was born. She narrowed her eyes, tried to focus on reading some of the words, but they swam in front of her. Stupid alcohol. She widened her eyes and tried again. Nope, she couldn't focus.

She put the notebook in her bag, got up and turned. The movement made her feel light-headed and she belched schnapps and Jägermeister.

Billy and Cal were laughing on the sofa about something. She wondered if Cal was telling Billy all about her and if that was putting him off. So what. There was damage everywhere. Who in this world wasn't damaged?

On the turntable, the guy was shouting about the devil and God and a monkey going to heaven.

She downed the last of her schnapps.

'I need to go home,' she said.

CHAPTER 18

Martha stood over her mum asleep on the sofa. Light from the television flickered over Elaine's face. She looked drugged.

Cal came in the living room. 'Zonked?'

Martha nodded. 'As always.'

Elaine took a couple of sleeping pills every night. Cal and Martha could've been having an orgy with a herd of elephants and she wouldn't have woken up.

Martha tried to imagine Elaine at a Pixies gig with Ian. Couldn't. Elaine now was frumpy and dull. Maybe that was Martha's future, watching late-night television alone and drugging herself to sleep.

She got a blanket and put it over Elaine. There was always a blanket handy, Elaine more often than not slept down here. She said she liked the noise of the television to go to sleep to. Martha thought it was maybe the double bed was the problem. Too big and too lonely. She felt a shiver as she imagined that in her future as well. Then she thought of Billy.

They'd left him outside Ian's flat, heading in the

other direction. She didn't know what he was expecting, or what she wanted either, but whatever it was, it wasn't happening tonight.

She and Cal jumped on the night bus, then got off a stop early so Martha could drunkenly commune with her heron. That's how Cal put it. The boy had no sense of nature. They walked the extra distance through Figgate Park. It was unlit, and they stumbled round the pond to the board-walk. From there you could see right over to Arthur's Seat. The heron was usually somewhere on the island. Of course, it would be sleeping now. The best time to catch it was at sunrise when it would sit on a small outcrop of rock at the edge of the island and soak up the new light with its wings hanging out, as if solar-powered. Martha imagined the bird now. It was an elegant thing, but Cal just laughed at her obsession with it, like he did most things.

Cal had a bottle of red wine in his hand. 'Nightcap?'

Martha looked at the clock. Ten past three. Shook her head.

'I'm off to bed,' she said.

Cal gave her a hug and they both headed upstairs.

She went to her room and threw herself on her bed. Exhausted. She rummaged through her bag and pulled out the notebook. Put the bedside light on and tried to focus, but still couldn't concentrate on the words spilling all over the page. She pulled out the printouts from the office, the stuff about Billy, Ian's obit, but she couldn't focus on that either. She stared at the picture of her dad for a while.

She got an interview cassette out her bag and slid it into the Walkman, plugged the headphones in. There was crackle and hiss, then her dad's voice in her head. It was an interview about a proposal to build a new school somewhere. Boring. The woman Ian was talking to was posh, complaining that the new school would ruin the area where she lived, that's why she'd organised an appeal against the decision. Local politics.

She found herself yearning for the small snippets of Ian's voice in between the woman's blether. Methodical, workman-like questions, attentive and functional.

And still alive.

She pressed Stop and removed the cassette. Raked through her bag for the other tape, today's tape. Found it, put it in and rewound to the start.

'Go ahead.' Her voice.

'Gordon Harris died this week in tragic circum-stances at his home, aged forty-five.'

Her body tensed up as she listened, waiting for the gunshot. She flinched when it came. Kept listening, her shouts, then Billy's. Then kept listening. The sound of a man half alive, the hiss and flutter and crackle of the tape.

Then something else.

A thud. Something in the background.

She was drunk. Maybe she imagined it. She

pressed Rewind and Play. Listened again. Not sure. Just noise. Maybe a car door closing in the street. Or a million different things. Or nothing at all.

She rewound and listened again. She was less sure every time. How much had she had to drink tonight?

She listened again. Hiss, crackle, rumble. Now she had no idea. She'd talked herself out of it already.

She sighed, switched the Walkman off and left the room.

Knocked on Cal's door.

'Yup.'

He was in bed drinking wine.

'Can I?' she said. 'It's been a bad day.'

'Sure, Munchkin.'

He held the covers open for her and she slid in, turning her back to him. He spooned her and she felt his familiar breath on the back of her neck.

She closed her eyes and tried to sleep.

GIG #1, 01/12/91

Elaine had never seen the Southern so rammed, but this was a special night. She was relieved she wasn't working. It was crazy at the bar, punters six deep.

The place was buzzing because of the gig. Not for the Joyriders, but the other band rumoured to be playing. She looked at the crumpled ticket in her hand:

THE SOUTHERN BAR
presents
THE JOYRIDERS
plus
VERY SPECIAL GUESTS
BENEFIT GIG FOR THE SICK KIDS
APPEAL
SUNDAY 1 DECEMBER 7 pm
THE SOUTHERN BAR, CLERK ST
£1 donation at the door

The ticket didn't give anything away but the flyers did. 'Very, very special American guests "Teen Spirit"' were playing. The flyers were handed out at the door of the Nirvana show down at Calton Studios on Friday. Didn't take a genius to work it out, which is why several hundred Nirvana fans had pitched up tonight. Apparently the band's tour manager was the brother of someone in the Joyriders, and they had a night off between shows.

Nevermind had only been out for a couple of months but the buzz around the band was everywhere. They were on the radio all day, every magazine cover, every late-night television show. Jonathan Ross's face was priceless when they tore through 'Territorial Pissings' on his show then walked off in a sulk.

They'd been equally violent at Calton Studios the other night, in a different league of aggression and melody. That's what Elaine loved most, the melody. These were pop songs dressed up as grunge. You found yourself humming them while walking down the street. That never happened with Mudhoney.

The Joyriders were just finishing their set. They'd arranged a semi-acoustic set-up in the corner of the pub, where the singer and bass player were now arguing. The bass player swigged straight from a bottle of Jack, the singer threatening to chuck him out the band. The guitarist and drummer were shaking their heads as if this happened all the time.

She finished her lager and stood up to get the round in. Waved her empty glass around the table, received nods. On her way to the bar, she picked up half a dozen more empties from tables. Force of habit. Also, it would endear her to Big Al.

She squeezed through the crowd, deposited the glasses on the bar and caught Big Al's eye. He nodded and began pouring.

She looked round the pub. Dark, sticky, noisy. Walls covered in gig posters – L7, Mega City Four, Smashing Pumpkins, local crap like Miraclehead and Cheesegrater. An old, knackered motorbike was mounted on the back wall. Everyone in black, lots of dreadlocks, tattoos. Everyone was getting tattoos and piercings now. Unthinkable a couple of years ago. She fingered the ring through her belly button, rotated it a little to make sure it wasn't closing up, a nervous habit.

Al was back with the pints. 'Seven ninety.'

She handed over a tenner and got change.

'Are they here yet?' she said.

Al shrugged. 'Haven't seen 'em. If they don't show, there'll be a fucking riot.'

She took the pints back to the table. Years of practice, four pints between two hands. Not a drop spilt, even with these crowds.

She got back to the table and put the pints down. An Eighty for Gordon, Stellas for herself, Dave and Gordon's new girlfriend Sam. Sam and Gordon were deep in conversation. Elaine wondered if Sam knew about her and Gordon's recent history. Bit awkward if she did.

She turned. Someone was in her seat. He stood up, grinning.

'Just keeping it warm for you,' he said.

He was six feet tall and had hair like Evan Dando.

Grey eyes. Cute, but a hint of darkness to them. He wore a Senseless Things long-sleeved top, one of the cartoon ones, drawn by the guy who did *Tank Girl*.

'It's crazy tonight, eh?' he said.

'Yeah.'

'Bet you're glad you're not working.'

'Do I know you?'

'I've seen you behind the bar before.'

'Did I serve you?'

He shook his head and drank from his pint.

She drank too. 'Didn't think so, I always remember a pretty face.'

He smiled. 'I'm Ian.'

'Elaine.'

They clinked glasses.

She never took her seat back.

They spent the next hour talking, cocooned by the crowd noise. No sign of Kurt. Ian was studying journalism at Edinburgh Uni and did subbing shifts down at the *Evening Standard*, covering weekends and holidays. He was flirting plenty. She flirted back. The attention was flattering. He was a sharp guy, not one of the Southern's regulars who talked to her as if she was a silly little girl. Creeps.

The Joyriders' singer got up on stage. 'I'm sorry, but it doesn't look as if our special guests are going to make it.'

Elaine looked at the clock behind the bar. Back of midnight.

The crowd groaned and booed as the singer

jumped off stage and disappeared towards the bar. The place almost emptied in five minutes. A lot of the punters were young enough to have school in the morning, Elaine guessed. A guy with a big chunky boombox left, no bootleg for him.

Ian went to the bar and she watched him go, checking out his arse. Couldn't make out much in his oversized jeans, but he was skinny, the way she liked. It felt good to run your fingers up and down a boy's ribcage.

A rise in punter noise made her turn. Kurt and Dave Grohl had just walked in, Kurt flicking hair out his face, Dave patting someone on the back in greeting. The guy from the Joyriders was over and talking, shaking hands. Rumour was he knew Kurt from supporting Nirvana years back in some post-punk outfit.

Everyone in the pub was looking at Kurt. Elaine wondered what it must be like, all that attention, never able to relax. He didn't look comfortable, fidgeting with his hair and pulling a thread on his tattered jumper.

Ian came back with her pint, nodding at Kurt and Dave. 'How about that?'

Elaine looked round the pub. Couldn't be more than forty people in the place now.

Ian and Elaine talked about music. Turned out they'd been to a lot of the same shows and clubs in the last few months. Elaine wondered why she hadn't noticed him before, and felt a growing sense of serendipity.

Kurt and Dave got on stage and picked up acoustic guitars. They didn't announce themselves, just started playing. The first tune was a Shonen Knife cover. Then 'Polly'. She loved 'Polly', so messed up.

They played seven songs, despite the crowd going mental for more. They ended with 'Come as You Are' and left the stage, Kurt signing a few things then sloping off to the toilets, Dave heading for the bar and getting a round in for anyone close by.

'That's one to tell the grandkids.' Elaine regretted it as soon as it was out her mouth, what a stupid thing to say.

Ian laughed. 'Yeah.'

She finished her pint to give herself something to do for a moment. She looked behind the bar. It was past closing time already, but Big Al hadn't rung the bell, which meant a lock-in. Could be a long one.

'Want another?'

Ian looked at his watch. 'I better not, they're giving me a trial run as a trainee reporter on the crime desk tomorrow.'

Elaine looked at him. She'd been giving him pretty clear signals that she was interested, and he was going home. Playing hard to get, really? She was falling for it, though, falling for him.

'I'd like to see you again,' she said.

'Me too.'

'What time do you finish at the paper tomorrow?'

'Eight.'

'Where's the office?'

'North Bridge.'

She nodded. 'Why don't you pop in here afterwards? I'm on from seven.'

'Cool.'

They both had stupid grins on their faces.

'See you tomorrow,' he said.

She moved closer and kissed him on the cheek. 'Yeah, see you tomorrow.'

He waved as he left the pub and she waved back, then she felt a tap on her shoulder.

It was Kurt. 'Excuse me, have you got any Benylin?'

She stared at him. Cute, but not as cute as Ian. 'No, sorry.'

He shrugged and scuffed away to ask the next table.

One to tell the grandkids.

CHAPTER 19

Martha stood in the doorway of the kitchen looking at her mother's back. Elaine was at the sink staring out the window. Outside was fresh and clear, sunlight slicing through the wires radiating from the telephone pole behind the shed.

Martha needed coffee and toast. She'd woken in Cal's bed but he was gone. Cal was always gone, he would be at the gym or the pool or out for a run.

She was still in yesterday's clothes. Mistake. She didn't have many work clothes, so these would have to go in the wash straight away, ready for tomorrow. She slid out of the skirt and unbuttoned the blouse, walked into the kitchen and threw them in the laundry basket.

Elaine jumped when she realised Martha was there.

'Put some clothes on, will you? This isn't Spearmint Rhino.'

Something about standing there in her bra and pants felt defiant. Martha didn't like her body but she didn't want Elaine to know, wanted to show her mum what her daughter had become.

She poured some coffee. Radio 4 was on, *Woman's*

88

Hour. Martha hated Radio 4, especially *Woman's Hour.* All those posh voices telling her what to think, re-assuring her she was a worthy human being. Bullshit.

'Elaine, when was the last time you listened to music?'

'Don't call me that, I'm your mum.'

'Well?'

Elaine sighed. 'I have no idea.'

'What was it like before?'

'Before what?'

'Me and Cal.'

'Blissfully quiet.'

'Seriously.'

'Seriously.'

Martha took a sip, scalded her lips, too hot.

'Did you and Ian ever go to gigs?'

'Where's all this coming from, Martha?'

Martha scratched her arse.

'You never talk about the past,' she said.

'What is there to talk about?'

'The past.' Martha did the voice of a spoilt teen. 'Obviously.'

She didn't know why she was digging away at this now.

Something in Elaine had closed down over the years. Martha knew it, Cal knew it, everyone knew it. All this stuff, the old music in Ian's flat, every-thing that had happened with Gordon, meeting Billy, it suddenly made Martha want to open lines of communication again. They didn't talk much, her and Elaine. They had never talked much that

Martha could remember. It was as if Elaine had tried to become invisible, to blend into the background. She'd succeeded. Martha wanted to pull her into focus somehow.

'You haven't asked me about my first day in the office,' she said.

This was poking at a scab. Elaine hadn't wanted her to do it, didn't want her to be in contact with Ian. Martha could understand, Elaine thought she was being replaced as the parental role model. Truth was, neither of them had been that over the years. Martha felt like she and Cal had raised themselves. Cal disagreed, as always. And anyway, Ian was dead now, so no chance of contact unless she got a ouija board out.

Elaine began sorting through the dirty clothes in the laundry basket. 'How was your first day in the office then, dear?'

It was kind of a joke but not. That was Elaine's way of dealing with conflict. What had happened to her, that she was unable to tackle the world head on, without sarcasm or jokes or cynicism?

'Fine,' Martha said. She thought about not mentioning it but she wanted to get a reaction, something meaningful. 'Except a guy tried to kill himself while on the phone to me.'

Elaine straightened up, holding her back. 'What? On the news desk?'

Martha shook her head. She realised she would be telling this story for the rest of her life. It already felt like a parable. The Legend of Martha Fluke.

Remember that time when that guy shot himself on the phone? How we laughed all the way to the hospital.

'I was covering the obituaries. The guy who was supposed to be working the shift phoned in, gave his own obituary then shot himself.'

'Oh my God, Martha, are you OK?'

'Shouldn't you ask if he's OK?'

'You're my daughter, not him.'

Elaine looked like she might try to hug Martha, who held up a defensive hand. 'I'm fine. I saved his life, though, kind of.'

Elaine was standing there with Martha's dirty blouse and skirt in her hands, rubbing the material with her fingers. Out damn spot and all that. 'Tell me what happened.'

Martha was still in her bra and pants. It had been empowering before, now she just felt exposed. She took a glug of coffee. 'So I was covering for someone off sick and the phone went. The guy sounded stressed. Started reading an obituary to me. He got to the end, said it was his own obit, then bang, I heard a gunshot. No answer on the phone. So this guy Billy got his address and we went round there and he'd shot himself in the face.'

'Oh God.'

'I know. We went with him in the ambulance. They operated but he's in a coma.'

'That's awful.'

'Turns out this guy is the regular obituary writer, the guy I was covering for, Gordon Harris.'

91

Elaine gripped the blouse in her hand tighter. 'Gordon Harris?'

'You know him?'

Elaine didn't speak for a moment. Looked around the room as if searching for something. Loosened her grip on the blouse a little. 'I met him a long time ago. He worked with Ian.'

'So he knew Dad?'

'Years ago.'

'Anyway, his wife was all over the place.'

'Wife?'

'Yeah. Apparently he had a history of mental problems. Like, as if we don't know what that's like, eh?'

Martha was trying to make a joke about it.

'That's terrible,' Elaine said. She went back to throwing dirty clothes into the machine. 'You got anything else to go in here?' She was trying too hard to be casual.

Martha shook her head and downed the rest of her coffee in one. Went to pour another.

'Should you be going back into the office?' Elaine said.

Martha had been waiting for this. Elaine didn't want her there, had something against that place and the people. Martha had always put it down to antagonism towards Ian, but she wasn't sure that added up any more. Ian was dead now, so what the hell?

'I'll be fine.'

Elaine looked at her directly. It made Martha

realise her mother hadn't held her eye the whole time she had been telling her about Gordon.

'You don't need this kind of thing, Martha,' Elaine said.

'Please don't say "in my condition", it makes me sound pregnant.'

'You're not, are you?'

Martha laughed. 'No.'

'Because that's something else that could seriously affect . . .'

'Elaine, please, I'm fine.'

'Don't call me that.' She stepped forward and raised her hand to Martha's cheek.

Martha flinched and pulled away. 'And before you say anything, yes, I remember all the "previous episodes", and I know I have my appointment tomorrow, and you don't need to come because Cal said he would, OK, Mum?'

'You called me Mum by accident, isn't that sweet.'

'Look, Elaine.' That spoiled teenager voice again. 'I'm not some fragile little nutjob that you have to tiptoe around any more.'

'You don't remember the worst of it.'

'I hate that,' Martha said, her voice raised. 'I hate how you become the official historian for my fucking depression, like you own the facts of it. I have it, I had the breakdowns, I had the incidents, I had the fifteen different medications, the time in the loony bin. I remember, Elaine.'

'I know you do, sweetheart, I'm just saying . . .'

'Well don't. I'm not that person any more. I'm a big girl and I can look after myself.'

'I'm still your mum.'

Martha took a deep breath. Every conversation with Elaine seemed to end up the same way. 'You have to let me live my own life.'

Elaine backed off, poured liquid in the washing-machine drawer and switched it on. The room filled with the whoosh and whir of the drum spinning, the skoosh of water and soap.

'Says the woman parading around in her underwear, shouting and stinking of booze. Please put some clothes on, Martha.'

Martha saluted. 'Yes, boss.' She meant it to be sarcastic but it came out subdued. She headed out the kitchen and upstairs, thinking about tomorrow's appointment and hoping that Cal would go with her, even though she hadn't asked yet.

CHAPTER 20

Martha made straight for the grave this time. She wanted a quick word.

No wind in the oaks today, sunlight playing through the leaves. A tortoiseshell cat with a long tail trotted along parallel to her for a while. She thought of yesterday's wood pigeon, the notion of reincarnation.

She stopped at Ian's headstone and turned. She was being melodramatic. There was no one else in sight, but she felt like she was on stage, putting on a show. She was about to speak when she noticed fresh flowers on the grave, a small bunch of lilies. She reached down and picked them up. No card, no message.

Who would leave flowers, someone from the office? Did he have people who cared about him that she didn't know about?

Martha looked round the graveyard again. Couldn't see the cat any more, it had skulked away into a clump of trees by the fence. She felt like she was being watched. Stupid feeling, straight out of a cheap horror movie, the kind Cal subjected her to. Martha pictured herself as the idiotic damsel in distress – going out into the graveyard alone, against the advice of the grizzled old-timer at the local store who warned her about suspicious goings-on up at the old haunted cemetery.

She shook her head to dismiss the idea. Threw the flowers back down onto the turned earth at her feet.

'So, that was some first day at work yesterday,' she said to Ian. 'Is it always like that?'

She chewed on her lip and raised her eyebrows.

'Still got nothing to say for yourself, huh?'

She shook her head.

'What's going on at the *Standard*, anyway? It's a regular little suicide club down there. I know things are bad in the newspaper business, but come on. That's two of you tried to top yourselves in a fortnight. There must've been some fucking depressing pay and conditions in your contract. Or maybe your generation have just discovered how shit life is. Took you long enough.'

Martha turned away from the gravestone and looked around.

'Well, much as I enjoy our little chats, Ian, I've got somewhere I have to be.'

She noticed movement amongst the trees and got that feeling again of being watched. She imagined the soundtrack, atonal creepy notes building slowly, indicating a madman wielding a chainsaw just behind the nearest oak.

She jumped when the cat crept out from behind a tree and headed in her direction. It was padding straight for her, carrying something in its mouth. She pictured it leaping out of the branches of a tree and grabbing the wood pigeon by the throat, ripping it to pieces, tearing the life out of it.

But as the cat got closer she realised it wasn't carrying the wood pigeon, but a rat. The sight of the tail made her queasy. Something about that ropelike extension, the baldness of it.

The cat slowed. It had a submissive look on its face as it snuck the last few feet and laid the rat down in front of her, on top of Ian's grave. The rat twitched its front feet and jerked its head around, but it couldn't get up. Its throat was hanging open and the cat had made a mess of the flesh around its belly.

Martha gagged.

The rat began frantically thrashing its head about as the cat retreated. The cat looked first at her then at the prize it had brought her. She had to do something.

She stepped forward and placed the heel of her shoe on the rat's head. Heard the skull crush beneath her foot, and felt it up through her leg. Swivelled her heel to be sure.

She stepped back, dragging her foot on the grass, trying to wipe away rat brains. She looked at the cat.

'You are a sick fuck,' she said.

The cat looked pleased with itself as it jogged away.

Martha stared at the rat, its head a mush of fur

and brains. It lay on the grave like a superstitious offering from a primitive tribe. She should move it, but she couldn't touch it with her hands and she didn't want to get any more dead rat on her shoes.

'Jesus Christ,' she said as she turned away from Ian and strode towards the exit.

CHAPTER 21

As she got on the bus, she threw a random tape into the Walkman. A Spanish woman's voice, lots of reverb, then a riff. She looked at the box – Jane's Addiction, *Ritual de lo Habitual*. A guy with a squeaky voice shrieking over some funk-metal. Strange.

She pulled the printout of Ian's obituary from her bag. Smudged her thumb against the picture of him, pint glass aloft. Tried to imagine the decomposing corpse in the graveyard, or his smashed-up body underneath North Bridge.

She read the obit for the sixth time this morning.

Born: 13 February 1970, in Edinburgh.
Died: 17 March 2014, in Edinburgh, aged 44.

Sometimes the word 'colleague' just isn't enough. Ian Lamb, who died in the early hours of Monday morning after falling from North Bridge, was a distinguished colleague of everyone he worked with at the *Standard* newspaper, but he was so much more besides.

From his early days as a trainee reporter on the *Standard*'s sister paper the *Evening Standard*, through to his more recent days as an accomplished and astute news editor, Ian was a companionable and compassionate presence, always ready to listen to the usual workplace gripes, but also to provide vital encouragement to all around him.

Back in 1991, Ian was studying journalism at Edinburgh University. I first met him around this time, through a mutual love of the indie and grunge music scenes. Ian was a decent guitarist, I remember. He never treated that side of things as anything more than an interesting hobby, although by general consensus he could have made a career out of music if he'd set his mind to it.

In fact, that applied to most things about Ian. Ahead of anyone else in his journalism class, he landed a prestigious work placement as a trainee crime reporter with the *Evening Standard*, at a time when the newspaper industry was flying high and competition was fierce.

Ian was already working as a freelance writer, penning gig and album reviews, and contributing heavily to music fanzines and magazines both local and national, but he craved something more serious. His nose for news stood him in good stead at the

Evening Standard, where he rose quickly through the ranks of crime reporting and then news journalism.

He was responsible for breaking any number of high-profile stories at the paper over the years, from the Hearts FC tax scandal to the terrible revelations about the disposal of remains at Mortonhall Crematorium.

When a vacancy came up at the *Standard* for a news editor, Ian seemed the obvious choice. He brought to the role something of his dark sense of humour, as well as a down-to-earth quality that marked the paper's newsgathering for the subsequent years.

Latterly, Ian was less than enamoured with the way things were going within the newspaper industry in general, and at the *Standard* in particular. He was heard to comment on more than one occasion that in a few years all this would be gone, and yet he maintained impeccable levels of professionalism from the moment he entered the office until the moment he left.

Outside of the office Ian was an intensely private man, and mostly kept himself to himself. I suppose I knew him as well as anyone, and indeed it was he who first persuaded me to apply for a job at the *Evening Standard* where he was working, so really I have my whole career to thank him for.

Anyone who knew him knew that Ian was private for a reason. He had suffered on and off from depression over the years, and it occasionally hung over him like a cloud. In later years, however, he seemed to have found a combination of treatments that worked effectively at keeping his mood swings under control.

However, the overwhelming memories of Ian are happy ones. Consulting with colleagues here in the office, we were continually to be found laughing at recollections of his anecdotes and wit.

Ian Lamb was brought up in Edinburgh by his widowed mother where he was a bright and popular pupil at Sciennes Primary School then at Boroughmuir High School. He claimed it was his mother's proudest moment when he received an unconditional acceptance to study at Edinburgh University. The fact that he never finished his degree – instead becoming a full-time employee at the paper – always annoyed him, for her sake, but he was nothing if not a pragmatist in the workplace, as in life.

His mother died at the end of 1992 from a stroke, shortly after he began working at the paper, and that death always cast a shadow over Ian's life and considerable achievements, in his own eyes at least.

Nevertheless, in the two decades that followed, he carved an impressive life and career out for himself, creating a lasting impression not only on the people he leaves behind, but on the institution of the press in this country.

Ian is survived by his daughter Martha and by his son Calvin.

By Gordon Harris

It was well written but cagey. All obits were cagey, they hedged around the less savoury elements of the subject's life, but this seemed especially vague. Concentrated almost entirely on his work at the expense of anything else. Virtually no mention of his upbringing or early life. Martha wondered about that. Tried to think what Elaine had mentioned about Ian's life over the years and came up blank.

She liked that bit at the end, 'Ian is survived by his daughter Martha and by his son Calvin.'

Simple, direct, to the point.

She was a survivor, it was official.

It felt strange to be a survivor.

The guy on the tape was singing about being caught stealing. There were dogs barking all over the song. What the hell? Martha had been nabbed on the take once, eight years old. A Wispa out of McColl's. Everyone was doing it, it was a dare, a rite of passage. She was the only one got caught. Elaine gave her total shit for it.

Martha didn't get off the bus at the Bridges, she was deliberately two hours early. Instead, she headed all the way south to Little France, to the ERI.

To see Gordon.

She pictured his face, smeared across that room in Leith Links.

She didn't know why she was going to see a man in a coma.

She looked at Ian's obituary again. This time rubbed her finger over the byline, 'Gordon Harris'.

She switched off the screechy guy's band and slipped in that tape, the tape of her conversation with Gordon.

The bus stopped and started down Clerk Street and Newington as she listened, her hands tight around the Walkman, squeezing it, feeling the give in the lid, the springs on the hinge tensing and relaxing.

Bang.

Her shouting again. Silence. Then Billy. More silence.

Then that noise again.

It didn't sound right. Didn't feel right. Something was wrong with all this.

That's why she was going to see a man in a coma. To shake him awake. To ask him what really happened.

CHAPTER 22

Different nurse at the intensive care desk.
'I'm his daughter,' Martha said, putting on sad eyes.

Electronic click. She pulled the handle and was through.

Stood at the other side of the door waiting for it to glide shut. Pressed her back against the wall for a moment, closed her eyes and opened them again.

The light was dimmer in here, less stressful. The whir and hum of machines was louder, the constant buzz of keeping people alive.

Martha wondered what it would be like to work here saving lives. And watching people die.

She had a tension across her forehead. Pressed her thumbs into her eyebrows and rolled them downwards. Heard a familiar crunch and pop, like a stiff back having the knots massaged out. She wondered about that sound, what was making it exactly? Muscle, sinew, cartilage? A nurse would know, maybe she should ask one. She looked around. There was no one in the corridor.

She made her way to Gordon's room, fourth on the left. Stood in the doorway. Samantha was at the bedside, same as before. Martha wondered if she'd been home at all, to face the mess her husband had made. Maybe better to stay here forever.

'Mrs Harris?'

Samantha turned. All energy had drained from her face since yesterday and she gave off an air of deep sadness and resignation. She shook her head at Martha, an aimless, almost involuntary movement.

Martha walked towards her. 'I'm Martha, we met yesterday.'

Samantha shook her head again, more forcefully this time. 'I'm sorry, I don't remember.'

'I work at the *Standard*. I was covering the obit desk when your husband phoned in.'

Samantha's face crumpled a little more. Increments of grief.

Martha put a hand on her shoulder but it felt wasted and awkward. There was nothing here between them. Martha was worse than useless, she was here to pester and intrude and she knew it.

She took her hand away.

'I remember now,' Samantha said.

Martha looked at Gordon in bed. There was very little change from yesterday, except he seemed somehow smaller, like he'd shrunk away from the world. His face was still covered in gauze, the oxygen mask on, the machines pumping and wheezing.

Martha stared at his hand on top of the white sheet, where a drip was feeding in. The tape holding the tube had come away from his skin at one corner, and she reached forward and smoothed it down, then felt weird about touching his hand in front of his wife. Martha didn't know him but she felt connected. The phone call. The sound of it, the feel of it. She was linked to all this now, linked to him for as long as he remained alive. Maybe longer.

She pulled up a seat next to Samantha and laid her hands in her lap.

'How is he?'

Samantha shook her head. 'No change overnight. The machines are keeping him alive. Brain function is low. His body is still in shock.'

'But he'll come out of the coma, won't he?'

Samantha sighed. 'They say it's still too early to tell. I don't think they're very hopeful, but they're not telling me that.'

'I'm so sorry.'

Martha noticed a small bunch of lilies in a vase on the table next to the bed. She got up and examined them. Similar to the flowers on Ian's grave. Small, white flowers, the petals unopened. Weren't lilies supposed to be for dead people? She fingered the stems, looking for a card. Nothing.

'Lovely flowers,' she said.

Samantha stared at her, then the vase. She looked as if she hadn't noticed the flowers before.

'Who sent them?' Martha said. 'A relative?'

'I don't know.'

Martha smelled the flowers. Not much of a scent with the blooms still closed. She sat down again.

'How was he?' Samantha said.

'What?'

Samantha didn't take her eyes off Gordon in the bed. 'When you spoke to him yesterday. How was he?'

Martha thought about it. 'Very upset. Distressed.'

Samantha's head dropped a little and she closed her eyes.

Martha looked at the creases around the woman's eyes. So tired. 'How did he seem when you last saw him?'

Samantha shook her head. 'Fine, that's the bizarre thing. I mean, he's suffered from depression in the past, on and off, but not for years.'

'Maybe he was hiding it from you.' Martha found herself taking the other woman's hand in hers. 'That's very common for people suffering from depression, to hide it really well from loved ones.'

'How would you know?'

'I've suffered from it all my life. Diagnosed eight years ago, but I knew there was something wrong way before that.'

Samantha looked up. 'Really? But you're so young.'

'It has nothing to do with age,' Martha said. 'It's a mental disorder, that's all.'

Samantha sighed. 'I read all about it, the leaflets when Gordon was diagnosed, then weeks online, looking for answers. Buying loads of books, getting medicated, looking for alternatives.'

'That all sounds very familiar.'

'But that was years ago. There has been nothing recently, no signs it was coming back.'

'Like I said, maybe he was hiding it.'

Samantha pulled her hand away abruptly. 'And what am I supposed to do with that information?' Her tone had hardened. 'What the hell am I supposed to do in the face of that little nugget of wisdom?'

Martha put her hand up, placating. 'I'm sorry, I didn't mean any offence.'

'You have no idea what it's like,' Samantha said. 'The deceit of it all, the disregard for others, the selfishness.'

'Actually, my dad killed himself a fortnight ago.'

Samantha stared at Martha for a long time. Her breathing slackened and the fight seemed to go out of her. 'Then you do know.'

'I've felt suicidal in the past,' Martha said, 'and even I don't understand it. There's no point attributing rational thought patterns to people in that mindset. I think of myself when I was like that and it seems like a different person, a ghost almost.'

'A ghost,' Samantha said, like an echo. 'A ghost who somehow managed to get hold of a gun and keep it secret from his wife in their own home.'

Martha angled her head. 'You've no idea where he got it?'

'I never heard him talk about a gun. Ever. I certainly wouldn't have had one in the house, I told the police that.'

'There are apparently pubs in Leith where you can buy firearms.'

'You're saying it was planned, there was premeditation.'

Martha shrugged. 'I'm sorry, I'm just trying to work out what happened.'

Samantha rubbed at her eye. 'Why?'

Martha felt the tension return across her forehead, longed to push her knuckles into her eye sockets. 'Don't you want to know what happened?'

Samantha's eyes were wet now. 'I know what happened. My husband tried to kill himself.'

Martha thought about the cassette in her bag. The noise at the end of the phone call. She thought about bringing it up.

Didn't.

She got up and stood over Gordon's body. His chest was rising and falling softly, in time with the wheeze of the life-support machine. She caught a faint whiff of the lilies from the bedside table, just a tiny trace.

Samantha was sniffling into a tissue.

Martha touched Samantha's shoulder as she walked away. It felt like the most useless gesture imaginable.

CHAPTER 23

Martha stopped outside the hospital and sucked in air. Something about the sterilised atmosphere inside felt like it had petrified her lungs. She gulped in freshness, springtime. Her work skirt felt tight, the elastic digging into her flesh. She fiddled with it, running her fingers around the inside of the waistband. She kneaded away at her forehead, scrunching her eyes closed then blinking them open a few times.

She looked around. She was getting stared at by two old men in pyjamas, slippers and dressing gowns at the other side of the entrance. They were both smoking, cigarettes cupped into their palms against the breeze. One of them had a drip on wheels and was using the pole to keep himself upright. He had yellow fingers and a sickly tinge to the grey beard around his mouth. The other one was in a wheelchair and looked like death warmed up.

Martha stared back and they both turned away. She imagined what their bodies looked like under their clothes – cancerous cells eating away the healthy ones, hefty scars on chests or stomachs, pouches of skin, wrinkles, decay. We're all dying in our own tedious ways.

She was about to head for the bus stop when she saw Rose walking towards the entrance carrying a small bouquet of carnations. She had a self-absorbed look on her face, which lifted when she spotted Martha.

'Rose,' Martha said.

'Martha.'

Martha nodded at the flowers. 'Visiting someone?'

'Gordon, obviously.'

'I thought you didn't know him that well.'

'We knew each other back in the day.'

Martha raised her eyebrows. 'Oh yeah?'

Rose shook her head. 'Nothing like that.'

'So how come you're visiting him?'

Rose shrugged. 'I thought someone from the office should. And I didn't think there would be many offers to traipse out here, they're a hard-hearted lot down there.'

'Whereas you're full of the milk of human kindness?'

'Something like that,' Rose said. 'Why are you here to see him?'

'What makes you think I'm here to see him?'

Rose gave her a sceptical look.

Martha said, 'Why do you think he tried to kill himself?'

'Why does anyone?' Rose said. 'Gordon has had a lot of problems with depression. And maybe he felt guilty.'

'About what?' Martha said.

'We all carry guilt around with us, don't we?'

'Speak for yourself,' Martha said.

Rose laughed. 'I used to be just like you.'

Martha scrunched up her nose. 'What changed?'

'I grew up.'

'Is that why you're shacked up with a boy half your age?'

'Billy is just crashing in my spare room while he gets back on his feet.'

'Do you think it's wise having a criminal stay in your spare room?'

'Billy's never been convicted of any crime,' Rose said. 'And I know you like him, and he likes you.'

Martha looked down, spotted a smudge on her heel, the remains of rat brains from the graveyard. She cleared her throat. 'This isn't the playground, I couldn't care less if he likes me.'

'Whatever you say.'

Martha sighed. 'Oh my God, you're so annoying.'

Rose smiled. 'You are just like I was at your age.'

'If you say that one more time I'll take those flowers and beat you round the head with them.'

'That's the kind of thing I would've said.'

Martha shook her head and looked at her watch. 'I can't stand around here blethering all day, I need to get to the office.'

'The dead wait for no one, eh?'

'Whatever.'

Martha made to walk away but Rose touched

113

her arm. 'Just be gentle with Billy, OK? He's been through a lot.'

'There's nothing between Billy and me.'

'Women like us, Martha, it's easy to hurt the people we care about, that's all.'

She let go of Martha's sleeve and headed into the hospital, the automatic doors swishing and shushing.

Martha saw the two smokers staring at her again, faces scowling and closed.

She turned and headed to work.

CHAPTER 24

Martha sat at Gordon's desk and stared at the screen.

The obit in front of her had her welling up. She didn't know the guy, but he'd lived a long and satisfying life, and she could tell by reading it that there was so much love in his life, from family, friends, those he worked with.

The picture was the usual old white man, thinning grey hair, open-necked shirt – could've been anyone's grandad. Could've been Martha's grandad, if she had any left alive. Why did everyone in her family die so young? There was never a Fluke family obituary like this – eight hundred words of understated praise, heartwarming details like his job surveying the remote Canadian wilderness, or his time building schools in Kenya, or his national service in Saudi Arabia or his rumoured involvement in the disappearance of the Stone of Scone.

This was a life. This was grabbing life for all it was worth.

What did Martha have to compare? Several years of medication and treatment for mental illness. A

115

placement as a trainee journalist. Still living at home with her brother and her mum.

Then what?

She tried to imagine herself in old age, dying at eighty-nine, like this guy on the page in front of her, Derek Simpson. Some random guy she'd never met but whose life had reduced her to sniffing into a tissue and wiping her eyes. She tried to picture herself as an old maid, hair wispy and thin, knuckles swollen by arthritis, papery skin, bifocals on a piece of string round her neck. They could run a picture of her surrounded by frayed rugs and cats. She tried to imagine dying after a brave battle with bowel cancer, surrounded in her last moments by doting friends and family.

Nope.

Couldn't see it. Just couldn't see it.

She worked out that if she lived to be eighty-nine, she would die in 2082.

Jesus Christ, that was never going to happen.

There won't even be newspapers then. We will either have transcended to a higher plane of existence, or be living on Mars. Or more likely we'll have reverted to warring cannibalistic savages, shivering in caves against a harsh new ice age of our own making.

Martha took a deep breath and held it. Not the relaxation technique she'd been taught, but it sometimes worked. She wiped away the smudges from her eyes. She was supposed to be working, she had to get her shit together.

She checked through the obit again, trying to disengage from the subject matter and look at it objectively. Searching for typos, clumsy language, anything that might be dubious or get the paper into trouble. She triple-checked the dates of birth and death, the picture caption and intro, tidied up the edges of the columns, got rid of a couple of hyphens, made sure the text flowed through the page as smoothly as possible.

Done.

One dead man down, the rest of the page to go.

She looked at the clock on screen.

2.13 p.m.

Six more minutes and it would be exactly twenty-four hours since that call. She was surprised she remembered. She'd looked at the same clock on the same screen yesterday when the phone rang. Hadn't registered at the time. What else could she remember if she put her mind to it?

So it hadn't even been a full day since Gordon had done it.

Felt like years.

The phone rang.

She jumped.

Stared at it.

'You're shitting me,' she said.

Let it ring.

'Seriously. If this is . . .'

Deep breath. Picked up the phone.

'Hello, the *Standard* obituary desk, this is Martha Fluke.'

The sound of someone crying and sniffling.

Martha rubbed her fingers on the bridge of her nose.

'Hello?'

'I'm sorry . . .'

'Take your time.'

'It's about my husband.'

Martha had her pen and pad at the ready. 'Go on.'

In amongst the sound of snuffles and gasps, she heard 'Wallace'.

She put on her softest voice. 'Is Wallace his first or last name?'

'Surname.'

For the next ten minutes she provided a shoulder to cry on. Mrs Wallace's husband had finally succumbed to some form of dementia. He'd spent the last two years unaware of where or who he was, unable to recognise his wife and children, angry and aggressive to all visitors until the last two weeks, when he became serene and childlike.

Martha couldn't use a single word of this stuff – the manner of death was usually skirted over, especially something harrowing like this. No one wanted to read about Mr Wallace's years lost in the wilderness of his own frazzled brain. They wanted to remember the man who'd been instrumental in setting up a cookery school for underprivileged kids in Perth long before the modern-day obsession with cuisine as porn. They wanted to hear about his antics on his gap year, where he travelled to Australia and was almost bitten by a shark off the Great Barrier Reef.

Martha kept Mrs Wallace talking, thinking of what V had said about getting the bereaved to write the thing themselves. She made a few tentative steps towards suggesting it, but her heart wasn't in it. Wallace had died this morning, for Christ's sake, his widow wasn't in any mood to hit a deadline. Martha took down a few more details, then told Mrs Wallace that one of the paper's regular freelancers would be in touch to interview her properly. Truth was, Wallace wouldn't make more than a sidebar, if that. Depended who else shuffled off their mortal coil in the next few days.

Eventually Mrs Wallace hung up the phone, still sniffling.

'Didn't get the appreciation, huh?'

It was V next to her.

Martha shook her head.

'You need to try harder than that,' V said. 'You'll understand after a month, when they review the budgets and haul you into the office. Roast your ass.'

Martha shrugged.

The phone rang again.

'Busy time for dead people,' V said, not taking her eyes off her screen.

Martha picked up. 'Hello, Martha Fluke on the obituary desk. Can I help?'

Silence.

Breathing.

Martha felt a shiver. 'Hello?'

She heard a man clear his throat.

'Hello, sir, can I help you?'

V was rolling her eyes at the next desk.

Martha tried one last time. 'Hello? Is there someone there?'

The clearing of a throat again. Then a voice.

'Did you say Fluke?'

'Yes, Martha. I'm the obituaries editor here at the *Standard*.'

A beat. Another. This was like pulling teeth.

'You sound so young,' the man said.

There was something about his voice. Edinburgh accent. Something familiar, but somehow different.

'I've not been in the job long.'

'I'll bet.'

What did that mean? 'But I'm perfectly capable.'

'Martha Fluke.'

Martha rolled her eyes at V, who laughed and shook her head. 'Can I ask what you're calling about?'

Click.

Dial tone.

Martha held the handset up to V.

'Prick hung up.'

'Happens a lot. The bereaved are an emotional bunch.'

'He didn't sound very emotional.'

'They don't sometimes. Especially the blokes. Keep it bottled up, that's the macho Scottish way, right?'

'He kept asking about my surname.'

V turned away from her letters page. 'Yeah, I meant to mention that, you probably don't want to be giving your name out.'

'Why not?'

'Get a lot of nutjobs attracted to death. Makes sense to keep that information to yourself until you know the person on the phone is legit. That goes double for men. Perverts.'

Martha did 1471. Number withheld. She felt a tremor through her body but shrugged it off. People withhold numbers all the time, networks don't provide them, blah blah. But still.

It was something in the guy's voice. Familiar yet different. She couldn't put her finger on it.

V gave off an exasperated grunt. 'Fucking wind farms,' she said. She held up a letter she'd just opened. Covered in a red scrawl. 'Can't these assholes come up with anything else to moan about other than wind farms? I'd like to stick all their faces in the blades of a turbine.' She ripped the letter into confetti and threw it in the bin.

Martha checked her email. Two new messages about dead people. She began to read, but kept thinking about that man's voice, trying to work out what was so familiar about it.

CHAPTER 25

Billy came by her desk at six and put on his squint smile.

'Fancy grabbing a sandwich?'

Martha realised she hadn't eaten all day, that was one way of losing weight. Maybe by the end of her stint here she'd be svelte and willowy.

She looked at her screen then at V.

V waved at her. 'You know the ropes already, girlfriend. Pages are nearly set, we're ahead of schedule. Go break some bread with Loverboy.'

Billy stuck his middle finger up at V, his smile getting more lopsided.

'Don't tempt me,' V said. 'I will sit on that and break it off.'

Billy made a show of shuddering and Martha smiled.

'Come on,' she said, getting up.

As they headed downstairs to the canteen, Martha stole glances at the scar on the back of Billy's head. She had read about it. An emergency decompressive craniotomy, one of the newspaper reports had said. Otherwise known as a hole in the head to let the pressure out. She felt the pressure inside her own skull. Took a deep breath and thought about her ECT appointment first thing tomorrow. She still hadn't checked that Cal was going to come with her. Wasn't ideal that she had to come to work after, but it was doable. She had a few hours to recover at home. She wondered about trying to explain it all to Billy, but he would be just like everyone else – imagining Jack Nicholson in *Cuckoo's Nest*, thrashing around and biting down on a gum shield like a madman.

She had footage of herself from her first visit. They weren't supposed to, but Cal filmed it on his phone. She asked him to, so she would know exactly what they were doing. She'd been re-assured by all the doctors but needed to see for herself.

She looked serene in the footage. Under anaes-thetic, controlled voltage applied, end of story. No jerking spasms, no furrowed brow, no manic staring in wild-eyed panic. Just resetting the mind. That old IT joke about switching it off and on again. Worked nine times out of ten. Reboot your personality.

And the feeling afterwards, as if that heavy, wet blanket had been lifted from her mind. Like her body was a landmass after the glacier had melted and the water run off. All her senses were buoyed. She could smell things again. Only then did she realise her senses had been dulled by illness, by medication. She could smell the earthy stink of her armpits when she hadn't washed. She could smell when she was on her period. She felt alive again, back in the world.

'What are you smiling at?' Billy said.

'Nothing.'

They got sandwiches and coffee and grabbed a table next to the window, the Crags looming over them.

'I met Rose today at the hospital,' Martha said.

Billy chewed thoughtfully. 'There to see Gordon?'

Martha nodded. 'She had flowers. I thought she didn't know him that well.'

'That's what I thought too.'

'And you are best friends.'

'Don't say it like that.'

'Like what?'

'Like we're fucking. We're not.'

'Fine.'

Billy lowered his sandwich. 'What were you doing there?'

Martha shrugged. 'Just wanted to check on him. I feel connected, you know? I was the last person to speak to him.'

'How's he doing?'

'Not good. His wife was there.'

Billy was chewing again. 'You speak to her?'

'Yeah.'

'Anything?'

Martha shook her head. 'Not really. She doesn't think he's going to live.'

'Shit.'

'Yeah.'

'She have any idea that he was going to do something like this?'

'Don't think so.'

'What about the gun? Does she know anything about that?'

Martha shook her head again. 'Did you hear anything from the police?'

Billy pulled a sheet of paper from his shirt pocket. 'Yeah, but nothing exciting.' He unfolded the sheet. 'It was an Olympic BBM nine-millimetre revolver. It's a starting pistol, converted to fire live ammunition. It's easy, a two-hour job. About half the firearms the cops see are converted starting pistols. Means it was definitely bought in a pub or down a back street, no licence or anything. Only his prints on it, obviously.'

Martha took a swig of coffee. 'I think that's what Samantha finds hardest.'

'What?'

'The premeditation of it. He went out and bought a gun, that's a lot of hassle. That's not just a spur-of-the-moment thing like pills or hanging. He had that gun in the house for a reason. And he kept it a secret for a reason. That's pretty fucked up. Imagine if someone you loved did that behind your back.'

'Brutal.'

'Yeah.'

They'd both finished eating by now. Billy took a last gulp of his coffee.

'So, it doesn't look as if we have a news story,' he said.

'Doesn't look like it.'

'Shame.'

Martha raised her eyebrows. 'Sure, but it's kind of more of a shame that one of your colleagues tried to kill himself, isn't it?'

'Of course,' Billy said. 'I didn't mean it like that.'

Silence between them. The canteen was virtually empty. The whole building was virtually empty. This business couldn't last. Martha wondered how she would earn a living in the future. What would all the journalists do?

'Speaking of death,' Billy said, 'how's the obit desk going?'

'Depressing,' Martha said. 'I had a weeping widow earlier. And a weird guy who seemed obsessed with my surname, then hung up.'

Billy shook his head. 'Never tell them your name unless you have to.'

'So I'm learning.'

Billy checked his watch. 'I'd better get back, got some death announcements I could be prepping for tomorrow, get ahead of the game.'

'Yeah, me too.'

'What are you doing after shift?' Billy said.

Martha had been waiting for that question. 'V has twisted my arm to go see her wrestle.'

'Really?'

'Want to come?'

Billy smiled.

CHAPTER 26

Summerhall was packed.

Martha drank her pint and looked round. They were in a large concrete box, a former abattoir, apparently, still with some of the fixtures and fittings mounted on the walls – big, rusty rings cemented in place, chains and hooks hanging down. There were three hundred people in the room, arranged on cheap plastic chairs facing a wrestling ring in the middle. It was dark, with strobes flashing, and some cheesy death metal bouncing around, guitar riffs echoing and arguing with each other.

The crowd was made up of metal fans and comic-book geeks, plus some obvious friends and family of the wrestlers, kids with large foam hands. *We're #1!* The bar was doing a roaring trade. Martha smiled as she soaked it up. She had no idea this world existed, in Edinburgh of all places. The atmosphere was completely non-threatening, like a pantomime for grown-ups.

Billy and Cal were next to her, talking to each other. She'd asked Cal about tomorrow, he was cool to chum her to the Royal Edinburgh even though it was an eight-thirty appointment. Who the hell wants to get their mind reset at half eight in the morning?

Tonight was a good distraction. So what if she had a hangover tomorrow? In a stupid kind of way, she figured the ECT would wipe her hangover away too. So really, she had a free pass to drink as much as she liked.

That way madness lay.

She looked at the running order for the night. It was a mixed bill, male and female, six bouts between them. V was second up. Her wrestling name was Vengeance. The picture of her was awesome. In a black spandex bra and hotpants, with her thick black fringe and grimacing for the camera, she looked like Joan Jett raging on steroids. Her opponent was someone called Buttercup, who looked three stone heavier than V and had a Mohican, arms covered in tattoos and a thick waist exposed in a spangly gold outfit. Skull-crushing thighs.

Cal nudged her, eyes wide. 'This place is crazy.'

The death metal faded and a booming voiceover began rabble-rousing, getting the crowd hyped up. It was low-rent stuff but it worked. Martha found herself going along with it, ironically at first, but she got sucked into the call and response like everyone else. Billy and Cal were the same, whooping it up.

The first fighters came out to thudding hip hop. Wolf against Viper. Martha shook her head. Really?

Both guys had tidy beards and shoulder-length hair and were wearing tight shorts, sweatbands on their wrists and comical grimaces.

But once they got down to it, there was some serious intent. OK, it was pantomime, but Martha found herself admiring the athleticism of these cartoonish guys. She couldn't climb a turnbuckle and leap off. She couldn't do a forward flip through the ropes onto the concrete floor. Who was she to mock them?

'This is awesome,' Cal said over the crowd noise. 'You think Viper might let me check out his trouser snake afterwards?'

Martha pursed her lips. 'Come on.'

'Have you seen the muscles on these guys? And these outfits, man, they must be gay.'

In the third round, Viper got Wolf pinned for a count. He sprang up, beating his chest in victory. Wolf took it badly and broke a chair over Viper's head on the way out. Everyone roared.

V was up next on the card. Billy went to get beers before she appeared.

Cal threw Martha a concerned look. 'You OK about tomorrow?'

'I'm fine.'

'Should you be drinking?'

'I said I'm fine.'

Cal looked at her. 'You're taking the day off, right? You're not going into work afterwards.'

Martha didn't answer.

'That's nuts.'

'It won't be a problem. Last time I felt fine after a couple of hours.'

'If you just tell them, I'm sure they'll understand.'

Martha sat upright. 'I'm not telling anyone at the office about this. You know what people think when you say ECT.'

Cal looked away. 'Well, there might be a problem about that.'

Martha's eyes widened. She grabbed Cal's jaw and turned his face to hers. 'You didn't.'

'It was an accident. I thought Billy already knew.'

Martha slapped his chin away. 'Fuck's sake, Cal.'

'Sorry.'

Billy returned with the beers. He was smiling. But Martha knew he knew. So, what, he felt sorry for her? Thought she was crazy? Fuck that.

She took her beer and faced the ring.

The voiceover guy began again, whipping up the crowd for the second bout.

V came out to 'American Idiot' by Green Day. Nice touch. She was grimacing and laughing as she walked to the ring, then she did a few backflips once she got on the canvas and ended with a gymnast's pose. Wow.

Buttercup came out to 'Enter Sandman', punching the air and snarling. She was so much bigger than V.

Once the bout got going, it was just as dumbly impressive as the last one. Lots of theatrics, playing up to the crowd, gooning at the front rows. Martha

131

found herself screaming for V to get out of a choke hold.

V slipped the hold but she was tiring, hands on knees, chest heaving. Several rounds with this dumptruck had taken it out of her. A few more slams into the canvas and up against the turn-buckles and she was bumped down into a shoulder pin and counted out.

V and Buttercup were immediately up, embracing and waving to the crowd, both soaking it in. No animosity after the bell this time, all friendly girls together.

'V,' Martha shouted over the crowd. 'Hey.'

V caught her eye and waved. She had a broad grin on her face, despite getting beat. Her eyes glowed with something real amongst all the fakery, and Martha found that simple pleasure infectious. For a moment she didn't think about ECT, her dad's suicide, Gordon in a coma, Billy's damaged brain, her own synapses and neurons misfiring, and just soaked in the applause, imagining it was for her.

CHAPTER 27

The walls of the Royal Dick were covered in bleached animal bones and medical instruments, the pub having been converted from the old veterinary school along with Summerhall next door. Martha sat with Billy and Cal, swigging her Erdinger and imagining animal ghosts haunting the room.

V appeared wearing a ZZ Top cut-off, short leather skirt and knee-high boots. Cheers all round. Martha surprised herself by jumping up and hugging her. She felt V's firm muscles in her squeezed embrace.

'That was amazing,' she said.

'Thanks, Flukester.'

Martha introduced V to Cal and went to get the beers in. Billy came to help with the drinks.

'I can manage four pints myself,' Martha said.

'I'm sure you can,' Billy said.

When they returned to the table, Billy got a buzz in his pocket.

'What a stud your brother is,' V said, nodding at Cal.

'He's gay,' Martha said.

'Well, duh,' V said. She rubbed Cal's arm, making him laugh. 'Any guy this buffed is bound to be. Nice eye candy, though.'

Billy was looking at his phone. 'Oh shit, Gordon is dead.'

Martha touched the table to steady herself as the world went a little off kilter.

'Fuck,' V said.

'The obit guy?' Cal said.

V nodded.

Martha looked at Billy's phone. 'Who's that?'

'Rose.'

'What does it say?'

'He had some kind of massive brain seizure. No point keeping the machines on. His wife said they could pull the plug.'

'Shit,' Martha said. She slumped into her seat.

'You OK?' Billy said.

She nodded, an automatic response. She was OK. She wasn't the one who had shot his face off. She wasn't the one who had to go back to that house and look at the mess up the walls, soaked into the carpet, sprayed across the sofa. She wasn't the one who had jumped off North Bridge in the middle of the night, when no one was around to talk him out of it, making sure to jump at the most effective place to kill himself. She didn't want to kill herself, despite it all, despite the darkness and the pressure between her eyes.

She rubbed at her forehead, a pincer movement that made her wince.

She felt Billy's hand on her back.

'Don't.' She wriggled away from his touch. 'I'm fine.'

She picked up her pint and raised it. 'To Gordon Harris.'

They copied her. She took a big drink, loving the coldness of it in her throat, the fizz in her belly, and she wanted to feel alive.

CHAPTER 28

'What the hell is a "badmotorfinger"?'

Martha was standing in Ian's living room with the album in one hand, glass of whisky in the other.

'Sounds rude,' Cal said. 'Like a dildo gone wrong.'

The four of them were emptying out the dregs of Ian's booze shelf. Martha hated whisky but that's all there was left. That or Turkish brandy. V had made appreciative noises at the whisky bottle, but it just tasted like antiseptic to Martha. It was doing a job, though. She struggled to focus on the back of the album cover.

The other three were flumped on the sofa, passing the Ardbeg around.

Martha pulled out the inside sleeve of the album.

'Holy shit, look at this guy.'

She handed it to V, who nodded.

'Chris Cornell from Soundgarden,' V said, 'he's been in the wank bank for years.' She scanned the sleeve notes. 'Don't you know anything about grunge?'

She passed the sleeve to Cal, who gave a whistle.

'Oh yeah,' he said.

Billy shook his head.

Martha smiled. 'I'm sorry, are we upsetting you with our man-lust?'

Billy held his hands up in submission. 'Hey, I'm not saying anything, I'm outnumbered three to one.'

Cal gave the record back to Martha, who slipped the vinyl out the sleeve and put it on. She was beginning to like the tactile experience of Ian's old records – a physical thing to hold onto, a chunk of black plastic or whatever it was that made a comforting scratchy sound when you slapped a needle on it. How archaic was that, sticking a sharp point into a groove to make a sound. How the hell did they ever come up with that?

She realised that since Ian's funeral she hadn't listened to a single MP3 on her phone, just his cassettes and records. She was regressing to the Dark Ages.

A blistering riff leapt out the speakers, frantic drums and bass, then this stud Cornell screaming. He sounded good. In control.

'Wow.'

V got up to mooch around the living room.

'So do you break into your dead dad's flat a lot?'

Martha had explained to V about Ian back in the Royal Dick.

'Quite a lot, recently,' Martha laughed.

V shook her head. 'Haven't the neighbours noticed?'

137

Martha shrugged.

'We close the door behind us, they probably don't want to get involved. Maybe they think we're squatters and this is a crack den.'

'This is no crack den,' V said, 'I should know.'

Martha gave her an inquisitive look.

'What can I say?' V said. 'I've led a colourful life.'

A sludgy, sleazy riff was chugging out the speakers now. Martha caught a line: 'I'm looking California and feeling Minnesota'. Nice.

Martha touched V's arm. 'There's something I want to tell you.'

'Shoot, sister.'

Martha turned to Billy. 'You might as well hear this as well.' She glanced at Cal. 'Although I know you already know because of blabbermouth here.' She looked at V. 'I might seem a bit weird at work tomorrow.'

'More than normal?'

Martha smiled. 'I'm going to the hospital first thing for an appointment.' She stalled for a second. 'At the Royal Edinburgh.'

V looked nonplussed.

'That's the psychiatric hospital in Morningside.'

'There's a psychiatric hospital in Morningside?'

Martha nodded. 'I'm due for an ECT dose.'

'ECT? Like . . .'

'Please don't say *Cuckoo's Nest*.'

'OK.'

Martha's mouth was running away with her. Whisky-fuelled.

'It's nothing like that. It just resets things. Me and Cal both have depression, I've tried every medication going – nothing stuck. I always felt I was still suffocating. I get regular doses of ECT and it works.'

V took a sip of her whisky. 'Why the fuck are you coming into work after that?'

'It's no big deal, I feel fine after. I want to get on with things.'

V shook her head. 'Don't be a hard-ass, take the day off. I can cover, been doing it enough.'

'I want to work.'

'Are there any side effects?'

'A bit groggy from the anaesthetic, maybe some short-term memory loss.'

V held her hand up. 'Whoa, lady, there's really no need.'

Cal piped up. 'I told you.'

Martha looked at Billy. Thought about brains and minds.

'Maybe,' she said.

She plonked herself down next to Billy and clinked his glass.

Cal got up and began dancing with V to Soundgarden, a slow smoochy dance, both of them making a joke of it.

Martha turned to Billy.

'How's the hole in your head?'

He narrowed his eyes. 'You heard about that?'

'Read about it.'

Billy rubbed at the back of his neck.

Martha held his gaze. 'Must've been a crazy time.'

Billy shrugged. 'Don't remember too much of it, actually. Took a shitload of morphine.'

'You were on the Crags when it went on fire?'

'Yeah.'

'And there were guys shooting at each other?'

'Something like that.'

'Wow.'

He took a drink. 'You know, Rose saved my life.'

'Really?'

'I owe her everything.'

They didn't speak. The guy from Soundgarden was yelling about Jesus Christ.

'How did Rose know about Gordon dying?' Martha said.

Billy shook his head. 'She's a reporter, it's her job to know stuff.'

'But this is our story.'

'There's no story. A guy from the office killed himself, that's it.'

Martha thought for a moment. 'There's a sound on the tape.'

'What?'

'After he shot himself. There's a sound on the tape.'

'What kind of sound?'

'A clunk or something.'

'What do you think it is?'

'I don't know. That's my point.'

'You think it wasn't suicide?'

'It's possible.'

Martha refilled her whisky glass.

'Do you think you should?' Billy said. 'The hospital and all that.'

Martha took a drink and waved that away. 'I wish you could know what it feels like. It wipes away all the shite that's accumulated. You start again with a clean slate. It's about getting a second chance.'

Billy smiled. 'I know what that feels like.'

Martha leaned in and kissed his cheek. 'I suppose you do.'

GIG #2, 07/3/92

She wobbled as she left the Sarry Heid. Ian took her elbow and steadied her. That last joint had really messed with her head. They'd smoked it between the four of them on the walk from Queen Street Station, then nipped into the pub for a quick pint before heading across the road.

She pulled the ticket from her pocket as they tottered across the road, the Barrowland's neon frontage making her eyes throb. She looked at the ticket:

REGULAR MUSIC LTD
presents
SOUNDGARDEN
plus Special Guests
SCREAMING TREES
at GLASGOW BARROWLAND
Saturday 7 March, doors 7 pm
Ticket £7 plus booking fee

Next to her, Ian was walking with an odd limp. His idea of hiding a few joints in a cassette case in his shoe seemed pretty ridiculous now. The speed wrap she had tucked inside her pants was much less likely to get detected.

'You're walking like an idiot.'

Elaine turned. Gordon was pointing at Ian, his arm around Sam. They were inseparable. Elaine felt a twinge of something, not quite jealousy. She was happy Gordon had found someone after their brief knockabout together, but he and Sam were so boring these days, this was the first time they'd been out in ages. Sam was one of those girlfriends who locks down her man, takes him away from his mates, especially girl mates. She looked at Ian. She wasn't like that with him, couldn't understand women who were.

Ian gave Gordon the finger as he hirpled across the road, avoiding a taxi. 'He won't be slagging me off when he wants a toke.'

A guy was slumped unconscious against the wall of the Barras, another guy pissing up against Baird's Bar next door.

'Ian.'

Coming towards them was a woman with big hair and big tits, exposed in a low-cut top. She was hanging off a skinny guy in a Pearl Jam long-sleeve, peroxide hair to his shoulders. The woman was mid-twenties and had a look in her eye as if she didn't take any shit off anybody.

'Rose,' Ian said.

Elaine watched as they greeted each other. They didn't touch. There was something unsettling about that, as if they were consciously avoiding it. But she was being paranoid, it was the skunk in that joint. She wasn't that kind of girl. She trusted him.

'Rose, this is Elaine. Elaine, Rose is my boss at the *Evening Standard*.'

'Colleague, not boss,' Rose said.

Elaine noticed that Ian hadn't mentioned that she was his girlfriend. Stupid skunk.

'I've heard all about you,' she said to Rose.

'Jesus, don't say that,' Rose laughed. 'I dread to think what Ian's been saying about me.'

Her voice made it clear she didn't dread it at all. She was confident and sexy and had no doubt that anyone talking about her would only say good things.

Rose smiled. 'He hasn't told me much about you.'

'Not much to tell,' Elaine said.

'I'm sure that's not true.' Rose turned to the guy she was hanging off. 'This is Alex, he's reviewing tonight for the *Standard*.'

Ian nodded. 'I'm doing it for the evening paper.'

This was a hierarchy thing. The *Evening Standard* was at the bottom, then the *Standard*, then the Sunday paper at the top. Ian had explained it to Elaine, who found the pettiness pathetic.

'When's your deadline?' Alex asked Ian.

'Midnight.'

'You're lucky, man, I have to phone it in by ten. Probably miss the encores.'

To make tomorrow's paper, the review had to be written on the spot and phoned in to the office, five hundred scribbled words mumbled drunkenly from a phone box.

Gordon and Sam caught them up and were introduced.

Rose pointed at the entrance. 'Shall we?'

She walked in without waiting for an answer, her arse wiggling too much.

'You never told me she was so pretty,' Elaine said to Ian.

He put on an air of innocence. 'Is she? I hadn't noticed.'

Wrong answer.

But she was being ridiculous. She needed to get some more mellow grass next time.

Inside, the place was jumping but the Screaming Trees were struggling. Mark Lanegan looked fucked, holding onto the mic stand for dear life. The two fat guitarists made up for it, rolling around on the stage and going nuts, but Lanegan stood there, eyes screwed shut, looking like he'd just drunk a pint of his own piss. Even 'Nearly Lost You' sounded tame to Elaine.

She excused herself to brave the bogs. Rose trooped along and stood with her in the queue.

'How long have you and Ian been together?' she said.

'Three or four months.'

'Sounds pretty casual if you don't even know how long.'

Elaine frowned. 'Four months. What about you and Alex?'

Rose laughed and flicked her hair. 'That's just tonight to get on the guest list.'

A cubicle became free and Elaine went in. Pulled the speed wrap from her pants, unfolded it and dabbed some on her tongue. Felt her eyes ping open like a cartoon character's. Pissed and wiped, then left.

Rose wasn't around so she headed back upstairs and went straight to the bar. Three pints of lager and a JD and Coke for Samantha. She wasn't buying for Rose or her fuckbuddy.

Harder to carry the pints in these thin plastic glasses, the JD jammed between her fingertips. The house lights were up between bands. She looked through the crowd and spotted Ian, but he wasn't with Gordon and Sam. He was standing arguing with someone. She didn't approach them, but stood and watched, anonymous in the murmur of the crowd.

The other guy was the same height as Ian but broader across the shoulders. Better looking. Shoulder-length curly hair, high cheekbones, and even from here she could see he had sharp blue eyes. A Dinosaur Jr. T-shirt clung to him, revealing muscle definition.

Ian shook his head then waved a dismissive hand. The other guy was pleading, hands out in supplication, but Ian was having none of it. He shoved the guy on the shoulder and the guy just took it like he deserved it. He tilted his head to the side, trying to reason with Ian, who looked round as if he didn't want to be seen with this guy.

Ian shook his head then pushed past the guy and headed towards the bar, obviously looking for Elaine. She took a sip from one of the pints and stood watching the other guy. He looked crestfallen. Elaine's mind buzzed. This wasn't just an argument over a spilt pint, it looked like it mattered, like it meant something. The guy turned and headed toward the stairs.

She saw Ian at the bar, craning his neck looking for her. She headed towards him.

'Where have you been?' he said.

'Bogs then bar,' she said, handing him a pint. 'I couldn't find you.'

They both took a drink.

'What did I miss?' Elaine said.

'Not a lot.'

Maybe it was nothing.

'Where are Gordon and Sam?'

Ian nodded towards the stairs. 'Went to look at the merch stall.' He looked worried.

'Everything OK?'

He gulped his pint and looked at the place he'd been standing arguing.

'Maybe we should go,' he said.

'Why?'

'I don't feel great, too much skunk. I think I'm going to throw a whitey.'

He looked fine, and he never took a whitey.

'You'll be OK in a minute,' she said.

'I really think we should go.'

'You have to review it, remember?'

He glanced around.

'Let's just go and chill at the back,' he said.

They walked to the back of the hall, where he slumped against the wall behind the sound desk. She realised she still had Gordon and Sam's drinks, so headed off to look for them.

As she scanned the crowd, she kept hoping she'd see that guy again.

Eventually she walked right into Gordon and Sam up the back, huddled together.

The music and lights dropped and a massive cheer went up. Strobes flashing. The band strode out and launched into 'Rusty Cage'.

Elaine glugged her pint and stared at Chris Cornell. She decided not to go back to Ian, this was a good spot, she could see perfectly. She tried to soak it up and stop her mind ticking over.

She couldn't.

Halfway through, Ian appeared at her shoulder.

'You feeling better, babe?' she said.

He nodded and gave her an awkward kiss. She tasted of beer and skunk. He'd sparked up another one on his own. So much for having a whitey.

He was scribbling in a notepad now.

'Writing nice things?' Elaine said, nodding at the page.

'Of course.'

She looked around, wondering where the guy was.

Soundgarden raged through 'Loud Love' and 'Hands All Over' then sloped off. Lights stayed down for the encore.

'Think I'll phone this in,' Ian said, waving his notebook.

'I thought your deadline wasn't until midnight?'

He shrugged. 'I've got enough, might as well do it now. Don't want you hanging around for ages afterwards while I dictate it.' He put on a smile. 'I'll meet you outside, yeah?'

Soundgarden came back on stage, Cornell with his top off. 'Jesus Christ Pose' then 'Full on Kevin's Mom' and they were gone.

Elaine joined the sea of bodies swaying towards the stairs. Always a crazy bottleneck in this place. She looked around for Rose, and for the guy Ian had been arguing with, but couldn't see anyone she recognised.

She stumbled out the entrance.

'Elaine.' It was Rose behind her.

'Hey,' she said.

'Great show, huh?'

'Yeah. Where's Alex?'

'Doing the review. Ian too?'

Elaine nodded. Awkward silence between them. Loads of bams wandering around, raucous noise from the Celtic pub.

She saw Ian coming from a phone box across the street. He flinched when he saw that she was standing with Rose, then crossed the road.

'Ian.'

Elaine somehow knew who it was without turning. The look on Ian's face, a flash of fear. She turned and saw the guy from the argument.

Ian was paralysed.

The guy certainly perked up Rose's attention.

'Aren't you going to introduce me to your beautiful friends?' the guy said.

It was cheesy charm, but he had the charisma to pull it off, somehow.

Ian shook his head and sighed like a tired old man. 'Ladies, this is Johnny.'

Johnny took Elaine's hand and kissed it. She was dismayed that she actually felt a tingle of something at that touch. Ridiculous.

The guy moved on to Rose's hand.

'Your brother Johnny,' he said.

Elaine turned to Ian. 'You have a brother?'

Ian's face was full of apology.

'Not just a brother,' Johnny said, putting his arm around Ian. 'A twin brother.' He mugged putting his head on Ian's shoulder. 'Can't you see the family resemblance?'

CHAPTER 29

Parking was the usual nightmare, even at a quarter to eight in the morning.

Cal nudged his Mini round the rabbit warren of the Royal Edinburgh Hospital looking for spaces, but cars were already double and triple parked, blocked in or sprawled across chevroned spaces with big warning signs: PLEASE LEAVE FREE – EMERGENCY AMBULANCE ACCESS AT ALL TIMES.

Martha sighed in the passenger seat. They could take as long as they wanted to find a space as far as she was concerned. She knew this was for the best, but she was nervous.

She fingered the leaflet she'd brought with her, the one they'd sent with the appointment letter. She already knew all the ins and outs of ECT, this was her fourth set of shocks in three years, but she reread the introduction in an attempt to calm herself.

Electroconvulsive therapy (ECT) has been used in Scotland for half a century. It is viewed in the medical profession as safe, effective and painless, with a low risk of unacceptable side effects. Furthermore, psychiatrists believe it can save lives.

However, this view has not always been shared by the public; this is perfectly understandable. Much of what people believe about ECT comes from the way it is portrayed in films, television drama and documentary, where the purpose is often to entertain or to be controversial.

No shit. So much stigma attached. And yet it had been the only thing that had worked for her. Five years of different pills, each prescription less effective than the last. Feeling herself sink into a black hole. Then after reading stuff online and convincing her doctor, a feeling like no other after her first shock, someone punching the lights back on in her life.

She had her appointments record with her. Three previous courses, each consisting of six shocks, two per week spread over three weeks. Once a year, so far. Maybe there would come a day when it wasn't needed, or when the risk of side effects became too much, but for now this was the least dreadful solution, and sometimes the least dreadful solution can be pretty damn good.

'Fuck it,' Cal said. Even the Mini couldn't fit anywhere around here. Eventually he just parked on a double yellow on the outskirts of the hospital grounds and they got out.

Martha could use a coffee but she wasn't allowed.

Nil by mouth for two hours before treatment because of the general anaesthetic. Nothing at all to eat for eight hours, just fluids. So the whisky last night was OK. She probably wouldn't mention that to the consultant, in case he pulled the plug.

The Royal was Edinburgh's resident nuthouse. Not that such terms were used around here, very much frowned upon by those in the psychiatric profession. But it was a nuthouse.

Originally a Victorian sprawl, peppered with sturdy oak trees strangled by ivy and holly bushes, it had accumulated growths like the Elephant Man over the years, prewar pebble-dash here, sixties tower blocks there, miserable grey concrete of the seventies giving way to sickening bright colours on the newest buildings.

They walked past the Child and Adolescent Mental Health Services building, where she'd attended as an outpatient since the age of thirteen. All softly spoken counselling and role playing. Then the allotments and greenhouses for rehabilitating patients, then the psychotherapy department. A year of talking things through in there amounted to fuck all.

They walked past the mortuary. Martha didn't think about what was inside.

Then they were at the Andrew Duncan Clinic, whoever Andrew Duncan was. Probably some old mental guy. Through the automatic doors, down a gloomy corridor stinking of bleach and they were there, the ECT Department.

She liked how they didn't have the full name. Electroconvulsive Therapy. Even here, in the hospital, there was a stigma, they didn't want to talk about what went on beyond this door. Or maybe they were just saving on the lettering of the sign.

Cal looked at her. 'You OK?'

She nodded.

'You don't have to do this.'

She buzzed and was let in. 'You know I do.'

It was the nurse she liked, the Irish one. 'Colleen' on her name badge. Red hair in a feather cut, motherly smile.

Martha handed over the letter.

Colleen flicked through a box on her desk and came out with some paperwork. She handed over the forms on a clipboard. 'If you want to take a seat and fill these out, dear.' She looked at Cal. 'And who's your handsome friend?'

'My brother Cal.'

'Ah well.'

Martha sat down and went through the forms. Just checking on her physical and mental health since the last visit. She'd already discussed this with her GP last week, but she knew from over the years with the NHS there was nothing they liked more than triple-checking things.

She signed the consent slip last and handed back the forms. Colleen got up and took the clipboard through to a room behind her. Martha knew how this worked. From here into the prep room, lie down, needle in the hand, count back from ten. Then according to Cal's footage, into the treatment room. Plugged into heart-rate and blood-pressure monitors, and something that checked brain function. Then a couple of probes on the head, shoot a little juice across, bingo. No shuddering or jerking, thanks to the muscle relaxant and the anaesthetic. Like watching paint dry.

Colleen came back.

'The guys will be ready for you in a second.' She looked at Martha. 'Just try to relax.'

Martha put on a smile. 'This is me relaxed, believe it or not.'

Colleen smiled back. Martha wanted to hug her.

Cal rubbed her hand, and she let him. She shot him a glance.

'It'll be fine,' he said.

'I know.'

A middle-aged guy popped his head through the door. Martha recognised him from last time, the anaesthetist. He spoke to Colleen and disappeared.

'Let's get you going then,' Colleen said.

She showed them through, and Martha climbed onto a trolley. The anaesthetist gave Cal a look, but didn't say anything.

Another man was there with the anaesthetist, taller, side parting, air of authority. He didn't introduce himself but his badge read 'Dr Pardew, Consultant'. Martha recognised him from last time as well. He lifted the clipboard and stood above Martha. He didn't show any signs of recognising her. She supposed he must do this to a lot of people.

'Feeling fit and well?' he said.

'Fine.'

'Nothing to eat or drink in the last few hours?'

She shook her head and wondered if she stank of booze.

'OK, just lie back and relax.'

She felt the needle puncture her skin and slide into her.

'Now, count back from ten, will you?'

'Ten.'

She thought about Gordon with his face gone.

'Nine.'

She thought of herself in a secure unit, the one and only time she'd been committed, for her own safety, three years ago.

'Eight.'

She thought of her dad lying on platform 8 of Waverley Station, and what had led him there.

She was gone before she reached seven.

CHAPTER 30

A simple fog.
　　　A heavy pulse behind her eyes.
　　　Voices.
Her brother. Cal.
And that nurse. The Irish one with the smile.
She felt a hand on hers, rubbing. It felt spongy.
'Sure, your sister has freezing hands.'
'She's always had terrible circulation.'
'Cold hands, warm heart.'
'So they say.'
Then closer to her ear. 'Gently does it, dear. You're just coming out of anaesthetic.'
Possible short-term memory loss.
Short-term memory loss.
And headaches.
That's what the leaflet said.
She remembered that. A good sign.
She opened her eyes.
It felt embarrassing to be lying down with people standing over her. Cal and the nurse. Colette?
Possible short-term memory loss.
That smile.
'Do you know where you are, dear?'

Martha blinked a few times. Heavy eyelids. She stretched her fingers under the nurse's hand. Made a claw shape, then relaxed.

Muscle relaxant.

Relax.

She nodded slowly. 'Andrew Duncan building. Who was he?'

'I have no idea, love,' the nurse said.

Martha saw her name tag. Colleen. She was close.

'Just relax,' Colleen said.

ECT.

She remembered.

'How did it go?'

'Oh, fine,' Colleen said. 'Just take a few minutes, dear, stay lying down. I need to go and get some more paperwork. They're terrible for it around here. I'll be back in a minute.'

She bustled out the door.

'How you doing?'

Cal, over her.

She nodded. Her head felt light. No sign of a headache.

'Good. How are you?'

He laughed. 'I'm fine, Munchkin.'

Martha pushed herself onto her elbows and looked round. She remembered this room from last time. A good sign. The brown walls. RECOVERY ROOM 1 on a small laminated sign above the door. A recess in one corner had another sign: OXYGEN. There was no oxygen tank there. She remembered that too.

She remembered signing the consent form. Her head felt as if a breeze was blowing through it. What was that song about windmills of your mind? Old song. Had she forgotten that, or had she never known it?

She remembered thinking about Gordon and Ian and counting.

Very good signs.

She remembered about all the death, the obituaries, holding back the tears at the desk where Gordon was supposed to be.

Yesterday.

'You OK?' Cal said.

She looked around for a clock.

'What time is it?'

Cal checked his phone. 'Nine.'

Martha shook her head. 'That was quick.'

'They don't hang around,' Colleen said, coming back in.

She handed Martha another form to sign.

Martha signed, her hand slow.

Colleen checked her pulse. Martha felt she couldn't speak while the nurse counted in her head.

'Well, you're still alive,' Colleen said.

Martha snorted a laugh despite herself.

Her temples tingled, like a static charge. She scratched at the skin.

'That sore?' It was the consultant, through from the treatment room.

Martha stopped scratching and shook her head.

'How is our patient?' the consultant said.

Martha didn't know if he was talking to her or Colleen.

'Fine,' she said.

The doctor checked her eyes and ears, like doctors always did. What did they ever learn from that? She half expected he would make her stick her tongue out. The consultant had hairs bristling out his nose and ears. He wasn't old enough for that, only forty or so. And he had a wisp of chest hair poking out from the neck of his shirt. It made Martha feel sick to look at it trying to escape.

'You feeling OK?' the consultant said.

She nodded.

'I think she can get her cup of tea now, nurse,' he said.

Imagine not calling a colleague by her name. Martha wondered if he even knew Colleen's name. What an arrogant prick. God-complex bullshit, except this guy was only sticking two batteries against loonies' heads, hardly brain surgery.

'Good stuff,' the consultant said, already heading out the door. 'See you at your next appointment.'

Door opened and closed. Swish, swish.

Gone.

Martha swung herself off the bed and stood up. She wobbled. Her legs were weak, she felt heavy. Her body waiting to catch up with her mind. Cal put a hand out for her to take. She looked at it and shook her head, then headed for the door to Recovery Room 2. She remembered which way it was. A good sign.

Through the doors, Colleen headed for the kettle. 'Tea?'

'I could murder a coffee,' Martha said.

'Take a seat,' Colleen said.

'I'll stand, thanks.'

She wanted to walk it off. Active, rather than passive. Living through moving. She paced round the room. It was the same decor as the rest of the building – scratchy seventies furniture, brown walls, bleach smell, dreary as hell. Enough to send you mad, if you weren't already.

She got the coffee and gulped it as she walked about. Burnt her tongue, it was too hot.

Cal sat in a busted chair and flicked through a magazine, keeping an eye on her.

Martha gulped more coffee and put the cup down. She was full of energy now. Her legs worked and her heart pumped and her brain was clear. She wanted to do things.

'OK, I'm good,' she said. 'Let's go.'

Cal got up.

Colleen frowned. 'Are you sure, love?'

Martha gave a sarcastic and condescending nod of the head, then regretted it.

'Well, you know about taking it easy for the rest of the day, yeah?'

'Of course.'

Colleen turned to Cal. 'Make sure she does.'

'I'll try,' Cal said.

Martha picked her bag up and slung the strap over her shoulder. She heard the familiar plastic

161

rattle of the cassette boxes in there, and thought about the tape of her and Gordon.

She opened the door and Colleen followed, placing a hand on her sleeve.

'See you on Friday, then,' Colleen said softly.

Like it was a visit to the dentist.

'Yeah, Friday,' Martha said, and she was out the door, heading for the exit, Cal and Colleen exchanging a look.

CHAPTER 31

Back at home.

'Are you sure you're going to be all right?'

Cal was leaving to open up The Basement.

Martha was freezing. She hadn't had this reaction before. Her hands were trembling, her bones felt thin and brittle. She wanted him out the door as soon as possible so she just nodded, scared that her teeth might chatter if she tried to speak.

Cal shook his head.

'I'll phone in, someone else can do it.'

She knew this was just talk. He was the only one who had keys to open up, and the only one trusted by the owner anyway. He would have to go in.

'I'm fine,' she said.

She pushed him out the door.

'I'll call you in a bit,' he said, already getting his car key out his pocket.

'Don't bother,' she said.

'I will.'

She closed the door and went through to the living room. Got on her knees and clicked the ignition for the gas fire. An old living flame thing, but it did the job. She grabbed Elaine's blanket from the back of the sofa and draped it round her shoulders. Huddled next to the blue flames and the fake coal. What was the point of fake coal? No one was fooled.

She felt the heat on her face but her blood was still chilled. She switched the television on but turned the sound down. Jeremy Kyle. Horrible freak show.

She got her bag and opened it. Emptied everything out. Make-up, keys, phone, cassettes, Walkman, Ian's notebook, and the stories she'd printed off, the ones about Ian and Billy. The two men in her life. She laughed at that. One dead and one fuck-up.

No headaches this time, just this chill through her. Weird.

She plugged her headphones into the Walkman and shuffled through the tapes. Picked one out and inserted it. Teenage Fanclub, *Bandwagonesque*. Cool title. Sarcastic. Pressed Play. Feedback, lazy voice, chiming guitars. Very slack. She liked it.

Short-term memory loss.

She wanted to check. Remind herself. Did a mental inventory.

She had started work two days ago at the *Standard*. Gordon Harris had shot himself on the phone. She was working next to V. She went to see her wrestle last night. Was that just last night? Cal and Billy were there. Billy was the family announcements guy on the *Evening Standard*. Also the guy from the headlines a couple of years ago, the Crags shoot-out guy. Rose was a reporter. She didn't like Martha. Or did she? Martha's dad Ian threw himself off North Bridge two weeks ago. She didn't go to the funeral.

What else was there to remember? She had drunk Ian's drink cabinet almost dry. She was enjoying her dad's weird taste in music that she never knew about. All those cassettes, recorded from vinyl. He would've had to buy the TDK D90s, sit and tape the albums, write the track listings by hand. She could just click iTunes and it was there. So weird, how much effort went into life twenty years ago.

But Ian had never mentioned music to her.

She had a thought. Pulled out his obit, the one Gordon had written. Scanned through it again. Short-term memory loss. There it was, the mention that he was heavily into the Edinburgh alternative music scene. Really? She tried to picture the middle-aged man she hardly knew as part of anything alternative. Alternative to what, what did that even mean? Another word in the obit, 'indie'. What was the indie scene?

Had this been the same time he was with Elaine, and if so, was she into the same music? She never played music round the house. What had happened to these people?

She finished reading the obit. Survived by his daughter Martha and his son Calvin. They were survivors. Was that all? She was fed up of being just a survivor.

The heat from the fire was through to her bones now, but she kept the blanket wrapped round her anyway.

She read the name at the bottom of Ian's obit, Gordon Harris. Dead. Last time she'd read this, he was only half dead. Someone would have to write his obit. Was that her job now, to go back and talk to Samantha?

She thought about the recording of him. His voice, petrified of what he was about to do.

Teenage Fanclub were singing about a 'metal baby' now. Vocal harmonies piling on top of each other.

She picked up Ian's notebook and flicked through it. Remembered looking at the book twice before. That was good, everything coming back to her. The two times before, she'd been drunk. Wide awake this time, head full of light. She could read the scrawl no problem, wasn't as bad as she'd thought when drunk. Funny that.

She read a few entries. Nothing exciting, just the day-to-day stuff of his life. It was from 1992. Before she was born. He was already working at the *Standard's* offices, by the sound of it. Trying to get a career going in journalism, just like her.

She felt dizzy for a moment, something like déjà vu, her life telescoping back to her dad's, mirroring it a lifetime later. She really was following in his footsteps, for better or worse.

Maybe the dizziness was the ECT. She felt her pulse. Seemed normal. The heat from the fire on her face was intense but she liked it, felt as if it was peeling an old layer of herself away.

She flicked the page in the notebook. A very short entry about going to Glasgow for a gig. She laughed in recognition, it was Soundgarden. He mentioned Elaine, said they were with friends. She tried to imagine their friends in 1992.

Then something that made her blood freeze all over again. She reread it, wanting to make sure. His writing was a mess, but it was clear enough. She read it a third time.

'The only downer was that my brother turned up.'

Ian had a brother.

She never knew that.

Why had she never heard about him before?

She scrabbled through the pieces of paper scattered on the floor. Pulled out Ian's obit again. Scanned it. No mention of a brother. How was that possible? Gordon was a professional obit writer, he wouldn't make a mistake like that. Unless it was kept from him too. But he had known Ian for years, since way back at the paper.

More importantly, why the hell had Elaine or Ian never mentioned a brother?

She grabbed her phone and called her mum. No answer, just Elaine's monotone on the voicemail.

'Elaine, it's Martha. Call me when you get this.'

She hung up and called Cal.

He picked up after two rings.

'What is it?'

She could hear clanking of bottles in the background. A whirring noise.

'We have an uncle.'

'What?'

'I just read Ian's notebook. He mentioned a brother.'

'So?'

'Have you ever heard of our dad having a brother before?'

'No.'

'Don't you think that's a little strange?'

'No, we hardly knew the prick.'

Martha shook her head. 'That's not good enough. Listen to me, Cal. Ian didn't like his brother for some reason, that's in the notebook. Elaine has never, ever mentioned him in twenty years. Gordon Harris wrote an obituary of Ian that didn't mention him. That's the clincher.'

'Why?'

'You don't leave that kind of shit out of an obit, Cal. That's specifically what an obit is for, for rounding up someone's life and namechecking the family. All the family. Unless . . .'

'Unless what?'

'Unless there's something to hide.'

'Wait a minute.'

'Something big.'

'You need to take it easy, Munchkin.'

Martha had the phone cradled in her neck and was shoving all the stuff back into her bag. 'No, I need to do exactly the opposite.'

'Remember where you've just been this morning.'

'This has nothing to do with that. The side effects are memory loss and headaches, not imagining diary entries and realising your own mother has been lying to you for your whole life.'

Cal sighed down the phone. 'Maybe she had a good reason.'

'Like what?'

'I don't know. Maybe he died twenty years ago. Or emigrated. Or disappeared.'

'That's still no reason to write him out of history.'

'Maybe she wanted to protect us.'

'From what?'

The clanking down the phone had stopped. 'Listen, I'm coming home.'

Martha threw the blanket off her shoulders.

'Don't bother, I'm going out.'

CHAPTER 32

'Don't you get it?' Martha said.

V ran a finger around her black eye and shrugged.

'So your family has secrets, whose doesn't?'

Martha dumped her bag on the desk and shook her head.

'Not like this. Not that get left out of official obituaries.'

V looked puzzled. 'Sure, that happens all the time.'

'What?'

'You think we check everything?' She rubbed her hand over her bicep. 'If the family want something hidden it stays hidden. You wouldn't believe the number of euphemisms we use in this business. Obits are a total whitewash sometimes, trust me. I know you've only worked here two days, but even you must've noticed that.'

Martha had, but this was different. She logged onto the computer.

'What are you doing here, anyway?' V said. 'I told you to take the day off.'

'I'm fine.'

'Did you get the old . . .' V made a lightning fizzle noise and put her hands out like holding electrodes.

Martha rolled her eyes. 'Very subtle.'

'Well?'

'It went fine.'

'You seem a little hyper.'

'That's nothing to do with it.' Martha fixed her gaze on V. 'I'm not bipolar, I don't get crazy highs, just lows, so that's not what this is. I'm just thinking clearly for the first time in ages. I know this is important.'

V held her hands up. 'It's your life.'

Martha took a deep breath. On the bus on the way in she'd called Elaine four more times, no answer. She'd flicked through Ian's notebook, but hadn't found another mention of his brother.

She logged onto the copy system and searched for 'Ian Lamb'. There were hundreds of hits with his byline. He had written something most days in the years he'd worked here. She scanned down them, but apart from stuff by him, there was just Gordon's obit. Shit, Gordon. He would need his own obit now.

She went onto the local hard drive of Gordon's computer. Hundreds of different folders. She searched again. Three hits, different versions of the obit. She opened all three. Clicked the last two to the back and started reading the first. The text was almost the same, just a little sloppier. But then she read the last line.

'Ian is survived by his daughter Martha and son Calvin, and his twin brother Johnny.'

Her heart was a jackhammer.

A twin. Just like her and Cal. It ran in the family. She checked the second draft. It had been changed to cut him out.

'I told you,' she said to V.

'What?'

'First draft of Gordon's obit for Ian. Mentions a twin brother called Johnny.'

V peered over. 'Really? What does it say?'

'Nothing.' She thought for a moment. 'Except that he's still alive. A survivor.'

V nodded. 'Uncle Johnny, eh? Wonder why he got scrubbed from the rewrite.'

Martha checked the date on the file.

'Both versions were written two months ago, a day apart. Six weeks before Ian jumped off North Bridge.'

V sucked her teeth. 'Yeah, that's pretty common.'

'What?'

'A lot of us have our obits done already.'

'Really?'

'You want to make sure it's good. Do you want to read mine?'

Martha frowned. 'So you're saying Ian might've written this?'

V shook her head. 'Not his speciality. More likely Gordon spoke to him, wrote it, then showed him a draft.'

'So maybe Ian vetoed the mention of his brother?'

'Could be,' V said. 'Although that begs the question, why did Ian mention him in the first place?'

'Unless he didn't,' Martha said. 'Unless Gordon already knew about him. They both worked here from around the same time, didn't they?'

'No idea.'

'Isn't it a little suspicious that Gordon just happened to write Ian's obit for him a few weeks before he jumped off North Bridge?'

'Not if Ian was already thinking of killing himself. Sorry to be blunt, but that's the obvious answer. He was already thinking of doing it, so he wanted to make sure Gordon wrote something decent.'

'This doesn't add up. Where's Gordon's obit? Did he write one for himself?'

V pointed at Martha's screen. 'Have a look.'

Martha searched the system, then the local hard drive. Nothing.

'Why would he phone his in on the day, when he was premeditating enough to have bought a gun from somewhere? If he was ready to die, why not write his own obit?'

V got out her seat and rested her arse on the edge of Martha's desk. 'You're thinking too much about this,' she said. 'You need to go home.'

'No.'

'You're applying logical thinking to suicide,' V said. 'It doesn't work that way.'

Martha waved at V to get off the desk.

'We're getting off the point,' she said. 'My dad has a brother. I need to find him.'

Straight onto Google with 'Johnny Lamb'. Nothing obvious. Tried 'John Lamb'. Lots of sportsmen, musicians, a few American politicians. She checked the first version of the name in the *Standard*'s database. Again, nothing to shout about. Then the second version. Some junior footballer had loads of mentions in match reports. She switched the timeline from newest to oldest.

Top of the list was an *Evening Standard* court report dated September 1992. She clicked. Just a short paragraph, about the same length as the piece reporting Ian's death two weeks ago.

A young Edinburgh man was sectioned under the Mental Health Act yesterday and sent to Carstairs Secure Psychiatric Hospital for indefinite supervision. John Lamb, 22, was arrested on September 12th after a violent incident on North Bridge. Although North Bridge remained open throughout the incident, Market Street was blocked for several hours afterwards, and Mr Lamb was taken to hospital, along with one other unnamed person. At the hearing, Judge Evans said he believed Mr Lamb continued to be a danger both to himself and others, and he will be held in care until such time as he is no longer considered to be a danger to the public at large.

CHAPTER 33

'Holy shit.'

V raised her eyebrows. 'What now?'

Martha turned her screen for V to read the article.

V squinted at it and frowned. 'Might not be the same Johnny Lamb.'

'Oh come on,' Martha said. 'We both know what "an incident on North Bridge" means. Suicide bid. Same place Ian did it twenty years later. It can't be a coincidence.'

V rubbed her elbow and shrugged. 'So chase it up.'

'What?'

'You're the one wants to be the hotshot reporter, go investigate.'

'What do you know about Carstairs?' Martha said.

'Not much. It's a loony bin.'

Martha spotted Billy returning to his desk.

'Billy, what do you know about Carstairs psychiatric hospital?'

Billy came over and Martha got him up to speed.

'You think Johnny is still there?' Billy said.

'It's somewhere to start,' Martha said.

Billy pointed at the phone. 'So ask them.'

Martha Googled Carstairs. The website was all NHS branding and corporate speak. It was just called the State Hospital now, no mention of mental illness. Martha scanned the site for a few minutes, but whoever had written it had taken a course in flannel, everything was couched in vague language, impossible to glean anything. She eventually found a contact number and picked up the phone. Had a faint shudder at the touch of the handset to her ear, remembering Gordon's voice.

She dialled.

A Glasgow accent, middle-aged, female. 'Hello, the State Hospital, how can I help you?'

'I'm trying to find out if someone is still a patient there.'

'I'm afraid we can't give out that information over the phone.'

'He was admitted twenty years ago, but I've only just found out about it.'

'Like I said, we have patient confidentiality to consider.'

Martha rubbed her forehead and squeezed her eyes shut. 'I'm a relative. He's my uncle.'

'If you have the name and number of someone on the patient's clinical team, and if the patient has approved it, I can let you speak to them.'

The woman sounded like she got this all day. She was a rock.

'Well, obviously I don't have that information,' Martha said, 'or I wouldn't be wasting my time talking to you.'

'I'm very sorry, but I can't help you.'

She didn't sound sorry.

'His name's John or Johnny Lamb. Can you just look him up?'

'Maybe I didn't make myself clear,' the woman said. 'It is illegal for me to divulge that information over the phone.'

'OK, can you suggest how I might find out if someone is a patient there?'

'Under the Freedom of Information Act, anyone who requests non-personal information held by the State Hospital, subject to certain conditions and exemptions, is entitled to receive it.'

'Well I'm requesting it now,' Martha said. 'So fucking tell me.'

'All requests must be made in writing. By law, we must respond to requests within twenty working days, but we can ask for more details in order to identify the information requested.'

She was obviously reciting from memory.

'Twenty days? In writing?' Martha clawed at her face. Her blood felt overheated.

'I'm sorry, that's the best we can do,' the woman said.

'OK, thanks for nothing.' Martha hung up.

She shook her head at Billy and V. 'Freedom of information, we can apply in writing, find out in a month.'

'Or we could go there and see what we can find out,' Billy said.

CHAPTER 34

Half a dozen horses flicked their tails at a trough or chewed on the long grass. Behind them was a twenty-foot fence topped with tight spools of razor wire. Behind the razor wire, the prison hospital.

Martha was driving Cal's Mini, Billy in the passenger seat. They'd left the office and hoofed it down to The Basement. Cal was reluctant when she told him why they wanted his car, but he gave in, she would only get a taxi for two hundred quid otherwise. He told Billy to watch out for her. Gave him a look.

Halfway to Carstairs she got a call from Cal. She switched her phone off without answering, knew he would just be nagging her.

Billy spent the journey down the A702 on his phone, reading out bits of blurb from the Carstairs website, surfing around trying to find out anything about Johnny Lamb. He called someone he knew at the sheriff court, but the records of the John Lamb case were archived, so the guy couldn't get them easily without a written application.

What was it about the old days, when everything

had to be done in writing? Martha couldn't remember the last time she'd had to put pen to paper to write an actual letter. Stone Age stuff.

She pulled over to the side of the road to get a better view of the place. Anonymous low buildings, yellow and grey, built from the sixties onwards, with some new building work off in a corner of the grounds, cranes and diggers shifting earth.

The plan was that they didn't really have a plan. According to the website, you were supposed to fill out an online form to apply for a visit. That would be passed on to the clinical team, who would consider it, discuss it with the patient if appropriate, then get back to you in writing. In writing, Jesus, this place was keeping the pen and paper business going single-handed. Then you were meant to get an authorised pass with your picture on it.

But there were ways round, that's what Billy said, there were ways round anything.

Martha pulled the Mini away from the verge and headed towards the visitors' car park. The horses didn't raise their heads.

No problems getting a parking space, no sign of security yet either. Large NHS-branded signs: ALL VISITORS PLEASE GO TO RECEPTION.

They got out and looked at each other over the roof of the Mini, the sun glinting off the surface between them. Martha laid her hand on the car roof. The spring sunshine wasn't enough to warm the metal under her fingers.

'You think he'll still be here?' she said. 'After all this time?'

'I have no idea,' Billy said. 'Maybe he died.'

'Gordon's obit said he was a survivor.'

'A survivor?'

'As in "Ian Lamb is survived by".'

Martha thought for a moment then pointed at reception. 'You'd better do the talking. It could be the same woman from the phone, she might recognise my voice.'

Billy shrugged. 'OK.'

They went in. Another bland waiting room, beige furniture, cheap wooden reception desk. Martha knew from looking that it was the same woman she'd spoken to. Hard face, weathered beyond her years, spiky brown hair, clumpy body under blouse and skirt. Name tag said 'Brenda'.

Billy started talking to her. Martha hung back, pretending to examine a leaflet on 'Living with Schizophrenia', listening in to the pair of them. Billy was getting nowhere. She wanted to run over and grab the woman by her blouse and scream in her face. Billy was never going to get in this way, all the sweet-talking in the world wasn't going to win Brenda over.

Martha took a deep breath and put the leaflet down, then walked out the front door without looking back.

She walked to the nearest fence. Gazed up at the razor wire. Imagined what it must feel like to be on the other side of that.

181

A guy in a hoodie with a Rangers tattoo on his neck stood outside the front door, smoking a roll-up.

She walked away from his gaze and round the corner. Tried a fire exit. Locked. Walked on further, just a thin strip of grass and a worn, muddy path. The path meant that people came this way, so she followed it.

Round a second corner the path ended at another exit, this time with an electronic keypad and lock fitted. Three women in tabards were standing outside, sucking on cigarettes. They were all middle-aged with bad dye jobs, blonde, henna and some crazy purple. Heavy lines on their faces, years of hard graft and nicotine. She kept walking towards them and they glanced up at her.

'Excuse me,' Martha said.

'Aye, doll?' said the one with henna streaks.

Martha put on her little-girl voice, innocent eyes. 'I think I've got a wee bit lost. I'm supposed to be visiting someone.'

The woman took another drag, then pointed behind Martha. 'Reception's round that way, don't know how you missed it.'

'Thanks,' Martha said. 'Sorry, I don't normally lose my bearings, I'm a bit all over the place.'

She went to turn, then stopped. 'I'm visiting my uncle, maybe you've met him? Johnny Lamb.'

Henna smiled at the other two, who gave her a knowing look back. 'Oh aye, we all know Johnny

Lamb. Took turns cleaning his ward. Never forget a handsome face like his. You're Johnny's niece?'

Martha nodded.

'Fucking idiots,' Henna said.

'What?' Martha's heart hammered away at her ribs.

'Johnny got transferred, did they not tell you?'

Martha shook her head.

'Didnae look old enough to have a pretty grown-up niece, mind you. Have you visited him before? I huvnae seen you about.'

'No, I just moved back to Scotland after years away.'

'Don't think he ever mentioned a niece.' Henna was scratching her chest, remembering. 'Just a brother.'

'That'll be my dad, Ian.'

'Ian, aye, that's right.' Henna turned to the others. 'The brother came to visit a few times recently, didn't he?'

The blonde one nodded.

Martha's throat was dry. 'How recently?'

'Up until Johnny got transferred,' Blondie said. 'Around Christmas time.'

'Where was he transferred to?'

Blondie narrowed her eyes. 'Surely your dad would've told you?'

Martha put on a sorry face. She was really hamming it up. 'We don't get on, me and my dad, haven't spoken in two years.'

The three women looked as if they understood bad fathers all too well.

'My old man was a bastard, too,' Henna said. 'But take it from me, you'll want to make it up between yeh afore it's too late. My da's deid now.'

'Do you know where Johnny was transferred to?'

They all shook their heads.

'His brother signed off on it,' Blondie said, 'at least that's what Johnny said anyway, so it'll be the nearest psychiatric hospital to where your da lives, probably.'

'Royal Edinburgh, would that make sense?'

'Could be,' Henna said, throwing her fag butt into the grass. 'Sounds like you've had a wasted journey. Idiots in this place dinnae know their arses from their elbows.'

Martha put on a big smile. 'Well, thanks for all your help anyway.'

Henna shrugged. 'No worries, doll.'

Martha turned and walked away, trying to keep her stride steady on the muddy grass.

Billy was sitting on the bonnet of the Mini, scrolling on his phone. He looked up when he heard her footsteps.

'Where did you go?'

Martha unlocked the car. 'Just for a mooch around. How did you get on at reception?'

Billy shook his head as he got up. 'Totally stonewalled.'

'Lucky one of us got somewhere then.' She couldn't stop grinning.

Billy looked at her. 'What?'

Martha waved behind her. 'Got chatting to some cleaners on a fag break. They used to clean Johnny's ward.'

'Used to? So he's dead?'

'Still alive, but he's been moved.'

'Where?'

'Royal Edinburgh, most likely. My dad signed the paperwork.'

'When was this?'

'A few weeks ago.'

Martha got into the car and Billy followed. Inside, Martha looked at him closely. 'I know I'm new to this reporting thing, but this is all pretty suspect, yeah?'

'Yeah.'

Martha turned the engine on and revved. 'That's what I thought.' She took a deep breath. 'I was just there, as well.'

'Where?'

'The Royal. That's where I got the ECT this morning. It's the only psychiatric hospital in Edinburgh. Because Ian approved his release Johnny would've been sent there, at least that's what my cleaning woman reckoned.'

'So, what now?'

'We go to the Royal.'

CHAPTER 35

They'd just hit the bypass when Billy got a call.

He pressed Answer. 'Hey, V, what's up?'

Martha was dealing with chaotic traffic, rush hour where the M9 fed into the ring road. Lane-switching all over the place. She glanced over and saw Billy frown.

'What is it?' she said. 'Are we in trouble?'

Billy held his hand up to her.

'OK, I'll tell her,' he said down the phone, then hung up.

He turned to her. 'Your phone's off.'

'I know.'

'Cal has been trying to call you for hours.'

A taxi cut in front of them, making Martha swerve across the lanes. A Tesco lorry tooted at her.

'Yeah, yeah,' she said to the mirror, then to Billy: 'What does Cal want?'

'Eventually he called the office, spoke to V.'

'What is it, Billy? You're scaring me.'

'Don't flip out.'

'What?'

'It's your house.'

Martha shuddered the car forward a few yards, easing into traffic. She frowned. 'My house?'

'It's on fire.'

CHAPTER 36

They saw the smoke from about a mile away. Then closer, the smell. Acrid, poisonous, choking, even with the car windows up.

'Come on.' Martha spoke to herself as she pushed her knuckles into her eye sockets.

They were sitting at a red light at the Jewel, a few minutes away.

She revved the engine. 'Fucking Edinburgh traffic.'

Billy touched the dashboard. 'Take it easy.'

'Don't tell me to take it easy,' Martha said. 'My home's burning down.'

Green light.

She swerved to overtake a Volvo and Billy's touch on the dashboard became heavier. 'Jesus,' he said.

They turned then turned again, Billy thrown about in the passenger seat, then they were in Hamilton Terrace. Round the final corner into Hamilton Drive and Martha slammed on the brakes. Couldn't go any further, three fire engines blocking the road.

All three had hoses unreeled and were blasting water onto the house. Smoke was pummelling out the windows in a rush to escape, flames licking out like winking eyes. Part of the roof was already gone, collapsed from the heat. Flames and smoke danced out the holes. The windows were all gone, blown out or caved in. One fire engine had a guy up a ladder, spraying onto the roof, the second one was aiming at the upstairs, the final guy was blasting water in through the living-room window frame.

The three guys working the hoses were in full heat-protection gear, arms and legs thick with padding, gas masks and helmets. Other firemen were busying themselves with checking the hoses, but a few were just standing around. Martha wondered what the hell they could be doing, surely they should at least make themselves look busy.

A crowd had gathered. Martha recognised the old guy, Fergus, from number 19 with his dog, Betty. The dog was cowering behind his legs. She saw other neighbours, people she said hello to in the street, standing around transfixed by the blaze.

She jumped out the car then didn't know what to do. Run to the house? What for?

She remembered sitting on the living-room floor this morning, the gas fire on, the blanket wrapped round her.

Had she turned the fire off? What about the blanket?

Where were Elaine and Cal?

She wanted to run in the opposite direction,

through the park, find a quiet spot amongst the bushes, curl up and sleep forever.

She stared at the smoke, trying to figure it out. The thick billows of black tapered as they stretched into the sky, twisting into sinewy strands, infecting the air around them. The smell of charred wood and brick and melting plastic and scorched glass filled her nose. She put a hand out to steady herself, touched the roof of the Mini. Cal's car.

Where was Cal?

She staggered towards the fire. She could sense Billy next to her, but she didn't turn and acknowledge him, didn't want to see the look on his face, or the reflection of the flames in his eyes.

She felt the ferocious heat now, making the skin on her face flush. Her eyes stung and her mouth and throat were dry, sandy.

She tripped over the kerb and righted herself.

She got as far as Fergus, who touched her arm. 'Thank goodness you're safe.'

Martha was close enough now to feel the spray from the hoses. It was turning to steam as it hit the flames at the open windows. She could hear the water sizzling, mingled with the crackle and crunch of the fire destroying her home.

Fergus nodded beyond the first fire engine. 'Your mother has been worried sick.'

Martha followed his nod and saw Elaine staring at the house, arms wrapped around herself like she was cold. She couldn't be cold, the heat from the fire was overpowering. Elaine's face was radiant, lit up by the flames.

Martha watched her for a moment, didn't want to break this spell. She would have to go over and speak to Elaine and acknowledge what was happening and they would have to face up to the fact that their home and all their possessions were gone, disintegrating under the weight and heat of the fire, and the tons of water flooding into the rooms, battling the flames into submission.

The longer she put that off, the longer she didn't speak to Elaine, the longer she could still pretend she had a home.

Elaine turned and looked right at Martha, then ran over and put her arms around her.

'Oh, thank God,' she said.

She squeezed Martha tight. Martha felt the roughness of Elaine's jacket zip against her chin as she pressed her head into her mum's chest.

'We didn't know for sure,' Elaine said. 'Cal said you had his car, that you'd gone somewhere, but there was still a chance you were inside.'

She let Martha go and they both turned to the house, warm spray on their faces, like having a shower.

'Where's Cal?'

Elaine didn't take her eyes off the flames. 'Talking to one of the fire officers. He spent ages trying to get hold of you.'

'My phone was off,' Martha said.

Elaine took her hand, both of them still staring

at the house. A section of roof cracked then collapsed, sending a blast of heat around them.

Elaine squeezed Martha's hand, and it felt like Martha was a little girl again.

'Where were you?' Elaine said.

'Nowhere important.'

CHAPTER 37

They decamped to Fergus's house.

After the initial surge of activity, the outsized firemen in clumpy boots, the flash of their lights, the searing heat and choking smoke of the fire, after all that, this was the dead zone.

Cal and the fire officer had found Martha and Elaine holding hands. The officer suggested they might as well wait indoors, there was nothing they could do to help, and it could take several more hours to be completely sure that the fire was out. Then the forensic people had to go over the place, look for a cause.

Martha didn't think about that.

It felt like a betrayal to leave their home still burning in the street, like leaving a dying deer in the middle of the road and driving off.

But now they were sitting drinking tea.

Or rather Martha was standing, staring out the window, her tea cold.

Fergus came in with a tray of biscuits, Bourbons and those pink wafer things. Martha thought the idea of biscuits was obscene, this whole situation was obscene.

She couldn't see their house from here, but she could see the fire engines, the firefighters, a handful of neighbours still out there, though they were dispersing. And she could see smoke and spray, their home's death rattle.

'I can't stay here,' she said.

'There's nothing we can do out there,' Cal said.

'Tea and biscuits, though?' Martha said.

Fergus lifted up the tray, not realising she was being sarcastic.

Martha shook her head, as much at herself as him.

Elaine was on the sofa, mug of tea clutched in her lap, head down. She lifted her head and seemed to see the room for the first time.

She looked at Billy. 'Who are you?'

'I'm Billy, a colleague of Martha's.'

'At the paper?'

'Yes.'

'Were you with her today?'

'Yes.'

'Why was her phone off?'

Martha turned. 'It just was.'

Elaine frowned. 'I thought you were having the day off after the treatment.'

Martha rubbed at her temple. 'I got bored. Anyway, I wasn't actually at work.'

'Where were you?'

Martha thought for a moment. Not a good time to bring this up, but when was it ever going to be?

'Me and Billy were at Carstairs.'

Elaine looked confused. 'The mental home?'

'The State Hospital.'

'What?'

'It's what they call the place now. But yeah, the mental prison.'

Elaine still gripped her mug in her lap. 'Why were you there? I thought you wrote obituaries.'

'It wasn't work, I was looking for someone. Johnny Lamb.'

Martha watched Elaine closely, looking for something. A reaction, like a cheap soap actor.

Elaine stared at the wisps of steam curling up from her mug.

'Does that name mean anything to you?' Martha said.

Elaine stared out the window. Two firemen clumped past.

'Should it?'

'Yes, it fucking well should,' Martha said.

Cal turned. 'Calm down, sis.'

'I will not calm down.' Martha turned back to Elaine. 'Is there something you want to tell us?'

'I don't know what you're talking about.'

'Johnny Lamb, our dad's brother? Our uncle, who we've never heard about until now?'

Elaine was still staring out at the fire engines, face blank.

'Maybe now's not the time,' Billy said.

'Fuck that,' Martha said.

Fergus was cowering in the doorway, Betty behind his legs.

'Martha,' Cal said. 'Billy's right, now's not the time.'

'Then when is the time, Cal? It seems there hasn't been a right time to mention this in the last twenty years. Don't you find that a little fucking strange? Don't you find it just the tiniest bit weird that our mother never once, in two decades, felt the need to tell us we had an uncle in a psychiatric prison?'

Elaine put her mug down on the coffee table and got up. 'I can't talk about this right now.'

She walked towards the door.

'Wait,' Martha said.

'No,' Elaine said. She had tears in her eyes as she turned. 'I'm going to see if there's any of our home left.'

'We have to talk about this,' Martha shouted after her, but Elaine was already at the doorway, Fergus shuffling sideways to let her past.

Elaine walked out the front door and over to the guy in charge of the first fire engine.

'What the fuck?' Martha said.

Cal sighed. 'It's been twenty years, it can wait a few more hours, no?'

Martha turned to him, her eyes wet.

'He's not in Carstairs any more,' she said. 'He was transferred to the Royal recently. Dad signed for him.'

'Shit,' Cal said.

Martha gazed out the window. Elaine was gesticulating with the fire officer. Martha thought about

196

the gas fire, the blanket. Someone had mentioned forensic officers. She tried to remember. Short-term memory loss. The ECT. A long-lost brother no one talked about. She felt the crushing weight of it all and reached out to touch the glass of the window. It felt cold, and she couldn't imagine the heat just a few yards away, destroying twenty years of her life.

CHAPTER 38

Martha was raging drunk.

She sat in the middle of the room, surrounded by the mess she'd made.

She'd spent the last two hours rummaging through the contents of Ian's flat, turning out drawers, emptying shelves, frantically raking through piles of crap, looking for answers.

Cal and Billy couldn't talk to her.

She knew she was being stupid. Irrational.

She sucked on a bottle of gin they'd found in the back of a cupboard. Winced. Made a face. Who the hell still drank gin in this day and age? It deserved to die in the twentieth century, along with all this other old crap.

What struck her now about Ian's stuff was how dated it all was. That he was set in his ways might've been expected, but a Walkman still being used in 2014? Really? She'd seen a cassette player like his, a yellow version instead of red, on a school trip to the Museum of Scotland round the corner. A fucking museum. That's where Ian and his mysterious brother belonged, dead and stuffed, on display in some dusty glass case down the end of a disused corridor in a museum no fucker ever visited any more.

But that wasn't true either.

Because Johnny was still alive. Still in the land of the living, very much still with us.

At least she thought he was.

It had been too late to make enquiries at the Royal after the whole business with the house. She'd phoned and tried to use her insider knowledge as an outpatient, but she got nowhere with the night-shift nurse, and was told to call back in the morning when someone would be able to help.

Elaine had gone to a neighbour's house, Barbara at number 11. Martha couldn't remember Elaine ever mentioning Barbara before, let alone being best mates.

By the time the sun had dropped behind Arthur's Seat, the fire at their home was under control. What was left was a soggy skeleton of brick and rafters, gallons of black water pouring out into the gutter and taking their family history with it.

Nothing to be done until morning.

Martha and Cal had turned down the offer of a bed at Barbara's and had ended up here at Ian's flat. Might as well make use of the place, since they had nowhere to call home now.

As soon as they came through the door, Martha

began turning the place upside down looking for answers, for some confirmation that this Johnny character existed, that he was in the world, breathing and speaking and shitting and pissing.

She'd tried to speak to Elaine again. Nothing. A brick wall. That annoyed her more than anything, her mother using the shock of the fire to avoid talking about the past.

The fire.

Forensics.

Christ.

She drank furiously as she threw clothes, papers and other crap around. Cal and Billy tried to calm her, but everything they said made her more angry. Why did no one else take this shit seriously?

She remembered the notebook of Ian's she'd taken that second night here in the flat. She pictured reading it in front of the fire in her living room. The room that was now a blackened shell. She pulled the notebook out her bag and rubbed at the cover with her thumb, thinking of Ian's hands touching it.

It was all her fault.

She tried to think positively, tried to picture the reboot of her mind this morning, resetting the synapses. It had lifted the weight from her, but everything else, all of life, had swamped back in and suffocated her.

Johnny Lamb.

Johnny fucking Lamb.

She swigged more gin, made the face again. Her eyes were unfocused, her brain more so. Cal and Billy sat quietly on the sofa, watching her.

Johnny Lamb, why are you such a fucking secret?

GIG #3, 04/6/92

She sat alone in the Bull, a pint of Stella and a torn-up beer mat in front of her.

Ian was a selfish, thoughtless prick.

She'd been fixing her make-up forty minutes ago in her flat when the phone went. He was cancelling on her. Wasn't the first time either. Claimed he had to work on at the paper. Didn't mention Rose, but he didn't need to. She had suspicions, but she didn't want to be that girlfriend, accusing and paranoid. What was it Kurt sang? Just because you're paranoid, don't mean they're not after you. Or in her case, just because she was paranoid, didn't mean Ian wasn't fucking that big-titted bitch behind her back.

So, fuck him, she had come out on her own. None of her flatmates were around and there was no point asking Gordon and Sam, they never went out any more. She pulled the two tickets from her jacket pocket:

DF CONCERTS presents
AFGHAN WHIGS
plus Special Guests

at THE VENUE, EDINBURGH
Thursday 4 June, doors 8 pm
Ticket £5 plus booking fee

She looked at her watch, then glugged her pint. AC/DC on the jukebox, 'Highway to Hell'. This was an old-school rock bar, full of leather and tassels. Not her scene, but there was something honest about it. She gulped the rest of her pint and left.

Outside she sparked up a joint as she headed down to the Venue. A whole joint in a oner was too much for her, so she nipped it halfway, waited for it to cool and stuck it in her pocket. Pulled out a wrap and dabbed speed on her gums. Ran her tongue round her mouth, sucked at her teeth.

She headed inside, nodding at Big Ian on the door. It was hot and sweaty inside, already three-quarters full. L7 were playing over the PA. She liked that an all-girl grunge band was getting somewhere, but if she was honest, she wasn't mad about their tunes.

She got a can of Red Stripe at the bar, better than risking the watered-down draught.

'Hello, gorgeous.'

She turned.

Johnny Lamb.

She felt a buzz go through her.

She'd met him twice since Soundgarden in February. After that first encounter, she teased Ian about never mentioning him, and Ian had clammed up. The times they'd met, it wasn't intentional, Ian apparently set on keeping them apart. When she kept on asking, he mumbled something about Johnny having a dark past, being unhinged, but he never elaborated. Which only made her more interested.

She looked at him now, wondering what secrets lay behind that curly fringe, those sharp blue eyes. She was glad Ian was working late at the paper, tonight was going to be a good night.

She raised her Red Stripe. 'Hello yourself.'

He took the can from her hand and drank, handed it back.

'Thanks,' he said.

'You cheeky shit, you owe me a drink.'

'Fair enough.' He leaned on the bar and got served straight away by a girl with a Black Flag tattoo on her arm.

Cracked the two cans and handed one to Elaine.

'On your own?' he said.

'Yeah, your brother bailed out last minute. Had to work.'

Johnny shook his head. 'He works too hard.'

'Tell me about it.'

'Very serious boy.'

'Yeah.' Elaine looked around. 'You with people?'

Johnny followed her gaze. 'I was,' he said, waving vaguely.

'Shouldn't you get back to them?'

He threw a smile her way. 'They won't miss me. I'd rather stay here with you.'

She knew what he was doing and she let him, didn't close it down. Why should she?

She nodded her head towards a dark corner and walked. He followed. She liked the simplicity of that, the power of having a man in her control. She pulled the speed wrap from her pocket and held it out.

'Want some?'

He smiled again. He was full of smiles. She couldn't picture him doing anything crazy.

He took it from her. 'Don't mind if I do.'

He unfolded the paper triangle and dabbed at the speed, three quick movements, his tongue flicking in and out.

'I owe you now,' he said.

'You don't owe me anything.'

He held out his hand. 'Here.'

Two pills.

Ecstasy.

'I've never taken E before,' she said.

He raised his eyebrows. 'There's a first time for everything.'

She looked round at the crowd waiting for the band to come on. The Lemonheads were playing over the PA, not 'My Drug Buddy', that would be too perfect. 'Stove', from the album before, about getting a new stove and missing the old one. Except it wasn't about stoves at all.

She took the pill and placed it on her tongue, washed it down with a swig of Red Stripe.

He grinned and threw the other pill into his mouth, then held his beer up to her.

'Here's to a good night,' he said.

Afghan Whigs were so different from the other bands kicking around. For a start they wore suits and had short hair. They just seemed grown up, like men amongst the angsty boys of grunge. Greg Dulli's concerns were a league above the teenage troubles of Soundgarden. And they had soul. They played a Prince song, covered 'Heatwave', then, for an encore, did a heartbreaking version of 'Band of Gold'.

Elaine soaked all this up as the waves of euphoria swept over her. She knew it was chemically induced, but so what, weren't all emotions just chemical reactions in the brain?

Johnny smiled at her as the band left the stage.

'Amazing,' he said.

'Yeah.'

He was talking about the band, but maybe something else too. She wanted him to be talking about her.

She wasn't angry at Ian any more, he just wasn't a concern. She couldn't see how he could feature in her future.

Johnny, on the other hand.

She leaned in, grabbed his hair and kissed him hard. He kissed her back.

★   ★   ★

By the time they staggered out it was getting light.

The pill buzz had died down, but Elaine still had a warm glow in her stomach. They were arm in arm, laughing at nothing. She sparked up the half joint, took a deep drag and passed it to him.

Waverley Station was closed, so they couldn't cut through. Instead, they headed down Calton Road then up New Street. Halfway up the road there was a turn-off into a derelict car park. Elaine grabbed Johnny and pulled him that way, into the muddy half-light. They were right next to the train tracks here, just over a flimsy mesh fence, the car park overlooked by East Market Street to their left. Above, towering over everything, the arches of North Bridge.

She pulled him into a dark corner under one of the arches. The flap of pigeon wings far above. She was giggling as she kissed him. He responded. She pulled him close, stumbled backwards till she felt her back against the stone wall. She grabbed his arse and felt his cock hard against his jeans. She ran her hand under his T-shirt, felt his muscles. Felt herself getting wet already. His hand was on her breast. She took it and slid it down to her crotch, then moved it up and down till he got the idea.

She pulled at her own belt and unbuttoned her jeans and he slid his hand inside her pants. She grabbed at his trousers and undid them, pushed them down past his skinny arse. Felt his cock press against her. Took it in her hand and stroked it a few times, then pushed her hips away from the wall and slid her own jeans down to her knees. She took his cock and guided it inside her. Pulled back from kissing to look at his face. He was smiling, a simple, cute smile. He started fucking her, slowly at first, then faster, both of them still looking in each other's eyes. This wasn't a drunken mistake, this was real, something she didn't have with Ian.

She was close to coming. She wanted the release of it, the celebration of it. She felt it sweep from her crotch through her body, her legs shaky, her back arched, her mind empty. Then she felt him come inside her, his body rigid, breath held, eyelids flickering. She dug her nails into his buttocks and he shivered and placed his lips on her neck.

'Wow,' she said, out of breath.

'That's one way of putting it.'

She laughed.

She ran a hand through his hair and looked over his shoulder. The glass roof of Waverley Station shimmered in the pre-dawn light. Above, the shape of North Bridge dwarfed everything.

They walked up the Royal Mile and South Bridge, past kebab shops and chippies, drunks drifting home. They didn't talk about what had just happened. Elaine rested her head on his shoulder as they walked.

They turned into West Nicolson Street and stopped.

Ian was sitting in the doorway of Avalanche Records, next door to Elaine's flat. He had a bag of chips open on his lap, but he looked asleep.

Johnny turned to her. 'I'd better go.'

'Yeah.'

'Fancy meeting you two here,' Ian said, trying to push himself onto his feet. He was drunk. 'Want a chip?'

Elaine looked at Johnny.

Ian did the same. 'What are you doing here?'

'Just walking Elaine home,' Johnny said.

Ian looked confused. 'How noble of you. I meant, why are you with my girlfriend?'

Johnny tilted his head. 'We met at the gig, the one you bailed from.'

'Ian, what are you doing here?' Elaine said.

'Came to find you,' Ian said. 'Work went on later than expected.'

'But you had time to get drunk after.'

'I didn't know where you were after the gig. The guys from the paper were heading for a wee nightcap, so I went along.'

'Was Rose there?'

'Of course, she's part of the team.'

Elaine imagined she could smell Rose's perfume on him. But then what could Ian smell on her? 'Go home, Ian.'

He frowned. 'But I want to speak to you.'

Elaine shook her head. 'Not like this.'

She got keys out her pocket and headed for her door. 'Give me a call tomorrow if you remember.'

She turned to Johnny. 'Thanks for walking me home.'

'My pleasure,' he said.

She went inside, her heart racing, and left the brothers behind her.

CHAPTER 39

Martha felt Billy pressing gently against her arse. Morning glory and all that.

They were in Ian's bed. Vague sunlight bled through the curtains.

Billy was spooning her, his hand on her upper arm, his breath on her back. She pushed her arse against him. A signal. She pulled her pants down and reached behind to stroke his buttock.

He got the message. She felt him slip inside her and move slowly in and out. She did likewise. She was still half asleep. Tried to remember last night.

Had they?

They were now, anyway.

Billy's hand had slid down and was playing with her. She felt a warmth spreading over her as they moved in time. In rhythm. It felt good. Better than good. It felt like being home.

Billy kissed her back, her neck.

She tried not to think of her house, burnt to the ground.

Tried not to think of her dad, lying on platform 8.

Tried not to think of Gordon's missing face.

Tried not to think of Johnny Lamb.

She wasn't going to come.

Billy was.

She felt him come inside her, and she wriggled her arse in circular motions, the warmth still spreading through her body, but not quite there.

Next time, maybe.

She turned to face him.

'Wow,' he said.

She smiled, kissed him on the lips.

'We need to get going,' she said.

CHAPTER 40

The smell was the worst thing.

Somehow the sight of her home in ruins didn't hit Martha as much as the stench of the place, a charred oblivion that caught in her throat and made her gag. Wet charcoal mixed in with something nastier, the reek of smouldering manmade materials, melted plastics and fibres.

There were no wispy smoke trails bleeding up into the sky, just an oppressive blanket of slush-grey cloud reaching down from above, spread over everything, keeping the stink in.

A thin stretch of police tape was strung across their front path. When had the police been here?

Martha lifted it and went under, Billy and Cal behind her, all of them silent.

Her eyes were wet. From the fumes. Or maybe not.

The roof was a wreck. Black marks stretched upwards from every window frame, from the front door as well, the ghost of the flames that had reached for the sky.

No one else was around.

Martha went to the front door and stepped

inside. She felt tears on her face and wiped them away. She never thought she would care about bricks and doors and windows, but this was too much.

The walls in the hall were black except for a few corners where the wallpaper had only bubbled and blistered.

Into the living room.

Burnt-out sofas and a charred television with a cracked screen. Melted cables running out the back.

The area where the gas fire had been was just blackened space.

She tried to remember. The blanket. Ian's notebook. The fake coal fire. Her shivering. Finding out about Johnny and leaving in a hurry.

She turned away.

Cal and Billy stood behind her. Cal wrapped her in a hug as she felt her body shudder with sobs.

'It'll be OK,' he said. 'The insurance will pay for everything.'

She sniffed and wiped at her eyes with the backs of her hands.

'Will they?'

'Of course, that's what insurance companies are for.'

Martha pulled away from him, went over to the window frame and looked out. From here, the garden looked normal. If she angled her head just right, she could pretend none of this had happened.

An edge of glass clung to the frame. She pressed

her hand against it until a spot of blood appeared. She pressed some more.

Eventually she raised her hand to her mouth and sucked at the blood. All she could taste was charred wood from the window frame.

She turned back to Billy and Cal.

'I'm going to find Johnny Lamb,' she said. 'You coming?'

CHAPTER 41

Martha paid the taxi driver and followed Billy out the cab.

Outside the Andrew Duncan Clinic at the Royal again. Was it just yesterday she'd been here for ECT? Short-term memory blah.

She looked round, but didn't know where to start. There was no obvious reception area to the hospital, the place seemed to have grown like a commune, lots of little self-interested departments, no overarching structure.

So she went to the place she knew.

'You OK?' Billy said.

Cal was on opening shift at The Basement again. Before he left, he'd told Billy to look out for Martha. She was insulted.

'I'm fine,' she said. 'Come on.'

She headed into the building, turned towards the ECT room, Billy behind her.

Got there. Lights off, door locked.

'Shit.'

Turned and retraced her steps, to the exit of Recovery Room 2. Locked.

She squinted her mouth.

She headed back along the corridor, stopped at the entrance to a cafe and looked inside. Formica tables, plastic chairs, cheap coffee machine. Pockets of relatives, patients and staff all hunkered down against the early morning.

She spotted her. Got lucky. Colleen, the Irish nurse.

She walked over, Billy still traipsing behind her.

Pulled up a seat opposite the nurse. Billy did likewise.

Colleen looked up from the *Now* magazine she was flicking through, raised her eyebrows and smiled.

'It's yourself,' she said. 'How are you keeping?'

'I'm fine.'

Colleen frowned. 'You don't have an appointment today, do you? I've nothing in the book.'

Martha shook her head. 'It's not that.' She reached over and took Colleen's hand, looked her in the eye, tried to put on her most serious face. 'I need your help.'

'I really shouldn't be doing this.'

'I know,' Martha said. 'I appreciate it.'

'If I got found out, I could get in a lot of trouble.'

'I wouldn't ask if I didn't really need to know.'

Colleen tapped away at the keyboard, sifting through the hospital's filing system on the screen. A few clicks, some more typing into boxes. Martha looked at the screen but couldn't make sense of the spreadsheet gibberish.

'John Lamb, you say?'

Martha nodded. 'That's right.'

'Do you have a date of birth?'

'No. Wait, yes. They were twins. Thirteenth of February. Let me think of the year.' She worked backwards in her head. '1970, I think.'

More tapping on the keyboard.

Martha sensed Billy to her left and wondered what he made of all this. The ECT, the house fire, the missing uncle.

'Found him,' Colleen said.

Martha leaned in to examine the screen. She wanted a picture of him, visual evidence that Johnny Lamb existed, but of course the screen was just full of database information, patient reference numbers, doctors' notes.

'It seems he's no longer with us,' Colleen said.

'You mean dead?' Martha said.

Colleen shook her head quickly. 'No, no. I mean not a patient at the Royal any more.'

'But he was sent here from Carstairs, wasn't he?'

'Oh yes, but he was only here for six weeks, it looks like.'

'So where is he now?'

Colleen ran a finger along the screen, checking the details. She squinted at the small typeface.

'He was released into the care of Ian Lamb,' she said. 'That ring any bells?'

Martha and Billy shared a look.

'Yes,' Martha said. 'My dad.'

'Sure, I have an address here. Forty-two Drummond Street.'

The flat.

Martha couldn't get her head round it.

'And when was he released?'

Colleen raised a finger to the screen again. 'Says here it was the fourteenth of March. So, what's that, twenty days ago?'

'Is that the last information you have for him?' Billy asked. 'No outpatient visits or anything?'

Colleen checked. 'He was due for a meeting with the consultant last week, but it looks like he didn't show up.'

'Isn't there some sort of protocol for that? Shouldn't the police be informed?'

Colleen looked at him. 'This isn't a prison, son, it's a hospital. If he was signed out of here, then he was judged fit to re-enter society. If he missed an appointment, there's not much we can do.'

Martha was shaking her head. 'Christ.'

'Are we done now?' Colleen said. 'I'd like to shut this down, I don't want to get in any bother.'

Martha rubbed at her temple, trying to think. 'Yes, of course, thanks so much, Colleen.'

'You're welcome, pet. Try to take it easy, eh?'

'Yeah, I will,' Martha said.

'So what now?' Billy said.

Martha shook her head again. 'I have no idea.'

Colleen's finger was hovering over the mouse as she frowned at the screen. 'There is one more note on his file,' she said.

Martha turned. 'Yeah?'

'There's mention of an information request pending.'

Billy shrugged. 'What does that mean?'

'The hospital has to release non-confidential patient information under the Freedom of Information Act if we get an enquiry. We had a request in writing on March eighteenth that's still awaiting a reply.'

The day after Ian died.

Martha's eyes widened. 'Who from?'

'Rose Brown.' Colleen looked up from the screen. 'Mean anything to either of you?'

CHAPTER 42

Billy held the door open for Martha as they strode out the building.

'No answer on her mobile either,' Billy said.

'Try her flat again,' Martha said.

Billy pressed the buttons as he walked, put the phone to his ear. They were across the overcrowded car park when he shook his head.

'Straight to voicemail.'

They walked fast out the hospital entrance, heading for Morningside Road through the neat rows of Victorian sandstone terraces. Posh neighbourhood. Martha wondered what they thought of having a loony bin next door.

'What about the office?'

'Just phoned. She's meant to be on shift but hasn't turned up.'

'Shit,' Martha said. 'We need to find her.'

Martha flagged a cab on the main road and they jumped in.

'Take us to the Regent Bar in Abbeyhill,' Billy said.

Martha looked at him. 'The gay pub?'

'It's the easiest direction to give. Her flat is right upstairs.'

Morningside Road was slow going. An old dear in front of them was making a hash of trying to park outside a little gift shop, holding everyone up.

'Fuck's sake,' said the driver.

Martha turned to Billy. 'So, you're the ex-crime reporter, what are we thinking here?'

'What are you thinking?' Billy said. 'It's your story.'

Martha pinched the bridge of her nose, then spread her hands out wide, inviting ideas. 'OK. Johnny was switched from Carstairs to the Royal a couple of months ago. After only a few weeks, he was signed out by Ian, three days before Ian jumped off North Bridge. We don't know where Johnny is.'

'And we don't know where Rose is,' Billy said.

'Correct.' Martha sucked her teeth. 'Gordon knew Ian, and knew that Ian had a twin brother. Do we think Gordon knew Johnny as well?'

'No idea.'

'And what about Rose?' Martha said. 'Why would she be asking about Johnny?'

'She knew Ian from way back,' Billy said. 'Maybe she knew Johnny too?'

A silence between them.

'OK, let's rewind a bit. Johnny spent, what, twenty-one years in Carstairs? What for? That wee article in the newspaper only said "a disturbance

on North Bridge". Must've been some disturbance, to warrant that sentence.'

Billy shook his head. 'They don't get a prescribed
sentence, not at Carstairs. They're just kept there
indefinitely until the doctors and whoever else
think they're no longer a threat to society.'

'So I guess good or bad behaviour while you're
there makes a massive difference?'

'As would the response from family members
outside, maybe.'

'Are you saying Ian might've had a reason to
keep Johnny locked up? What would that be?'

'And why would that reason suddenly change a
couple of months ago?' Billy said. 'After so many
years?'

Martha sighed. 'Where does Rose fit into all this?'

'No idea.'

'And what about Elaine?'

Billy just shrugged.

Their taxi was heading through the Meadows
now, past a bunch of students playing Frisbee.
Martha tried to remember a time when she was
just a carefree student, mucking around in a park
with her friends.

'We really have no idea what the hell's going on,
do we?' she said.

CHAPTER 43

Martha watched Billy pay the driver this time. This wild goose chase was costing them a fortune in cab fares.

They got out at the Regent and Billy fished his keys out his pocket. It was only then Martha remembered he lived with Rose. Strange set-up.

'Rose has some questions to answer,' she said.

Billy gave her a look. 'Let's just wait and see what she has to say for herself, I'm sure it'll all add up.'

In the front door, then up the stairs to the third floor.

Into the flat.

Billy stepped over a couple of letters on the floor behind the letterbox.

'Rose?'

No answer.

They headed through to the living room.

Nice flat. Newly sanded floorboards, high ceilings, tasteful bookshelves in distressed white. There was a beautiful view over to Salisbury Crags out the bay window. Must've been a great place to see them in flames the night Billy was up there.

Through into the kitchen, equally tasteful. Marble work surfaces, a classy cooker and utensil rack.

'Rose?'

Nothing.

Then they heard a soft thump.

Back out and down the hall to the other end of the flat. Rose's bedroom. The door was closed.

Billy knocked. 'Rose, are you OK?'

No answer. Martha looked at him, raised her eyebrows.

Billy pushed the door open.

Rose was lying on a double bed in silky maroon underwear. The sheets were ruffled around her, as if she'd been restless in her sleep. There was a small pool of vomit on the pillow next to her head, and a thin sliver of drool webbed from the corner of her mouth to it.

Martha saw a laptop open on the bed beyond her, but couldn't see the screen from here. There was an empty bottle of gin on the floor, and Rose's hand was hanging over the side of the bed above it. That had been the noise – the sound of the bottle hitting the floor. On the bedside table was an empty bottle of prescription pills, the lid lying neatly next to the bottle.

'Fuck,' Billy said. 'Rose?' He went to her and shook her. 'Rose.'

He sat her upright. Her head lolled to the side like a puppet with the strings cut. Totally out of it. Her breasts almost hanging out of her bra.

Martha pulled her mobile out and dialled 999.

'This is total bullshit, Rose,' Billy said. 'This is not you.'

He shook her again, then tried to prise an eyelid open. The eye was rolled right back, just the white showing. He put his ear to her mouth, then felt her neck for a pulse.

'She's still alive,' he said. 'She's breathing.'

Martha told the woman on the phone they needed an ambulance, told them the address, what had happened. She got put through to someone who asked what Rose had taken.

'A bottle of gin and a bottle of pills.'

'What are the pills?'

She went over to the bedside table and lifted the bottle.

'Xanax.' The prescription on the bottle was made out to 'Ms R. Brown'.

They told her just to stay calm, they'd be there as soon as possible, and Martha hung up.

'What did they say?' Billy said.

'To hang on till the ambulance arrives.'

'Is that it?'

'It'll be here in a few minutes,' Martha said. This was like last time, with Gordon, all over again.

'We can't just sit here.'

'What do you suggest?'

'We've got to empty her stomach.'

'You sure?'

'You've seen it on television enough. Help me.'

They took an arm each and tried to walk her

up and down the hall but her feet dragged behind her.

'Come on,' Billy said. 'Fuck's sake, wake up. You can't do this, understand?'

It wasn't working.

They walked her into the bathroom, to the sink, bent her over and Billy stuck two fingers down her throat. Martha's gag reflexes worked at the thought of it as Billy continued, removing his fingers and pushing them in again between Rose's pale lips.

'Is that a good idea?' Martha said.

'I've got to do something.'

Just then Billy's hand was swamped in vomit as Rose puked all over the sink and floor. Her throat spasmed as the puke was replaced by yellow bile. Martha saw undigested pills amongst the watery mess and wondered how many she'd taken.

Billy whispered in Rose's ear. 'Come on, wake up, stay with us.'

The buzzer went and Martha bolted to the door.

Two paramedics came in and hustled through to the bathroom, asking questions in steady voices. Martha showed one of them the pill bottle while the other spoke to Rose, easing her onto a stretcher and examining her.

'Let's move her,' he said, placing an oxygen mask over her mouth.

They lifted the stretcher and their bags of equipment and headed for the door, Billy following them.

Martha headed for the bedroom. 'I'll see you down there.'

She ran and scooped up the laptop from Rose's bed. Shoogled the touchpad to wake it up, but it was password-protected. She closed the screen and popped the laptop into her bag, then left the flat.

Downstairs they were getting the stretcher into the back of the ambulance, punters in the Regent ogling out the window at the activity.

Martha followed Billy into the ambulance. Their second ride in the back of an ambulance this week.

CHAPTER 44

This time they had a legitimate reason to be in the ICU.

It was the same nurse from before, when they'd blagged in to see Gordon. She gave them a funny look, as if they were cursed. Who goes to see two unrelated people in intensive care in the space of a couple of days?

Maybe the nurse was right, Martha thought. Maybe she was the Grim Reaper, bringing death to all those who came near. She would've laughed at the idea if it didn't have a ring of awful truth about it.

But Rose wasn't dead. Not yet, anyway.

The nurse buzzed them through, throwing them a scowl.

Martha wondered if Rose would be in the same bed, the one Gordon had died in. The deathbed. That would be a sign, wouldn't it? A sign that Martha was a harbinger of doom.

But it wasn't the same bed, her room was further along, on the other side of the corridor. Fate was never that neat.

There was a cop by Rose's bedside. Not a PC

Plod, someone higher up, judging by the stripes on the uniform. Hair greying at the sides, distinguished, but hangdog, his face tripping him. He was staring at Rose, laid out on the bed, white sheets over her body. She seemed somehow diminished, like she'd shrunk. Her face was a patchy grey, red blotches on her cheeks. Maybe the toxins were trying to leech out.

There had been stomach pumping at A & E, and a few injections. Martha didn't know what of. Lots of doctor chat about anti-this and haemo-that. Some mention of adrenalin. Martha had plenty of that to spare. In the end, they said Rose was stable but in a coma. Same as Gordon. Although the A & E doctor – a woman not much older than Martha – said Rose had a good chance of recovery. The coma was probably just the body shutting down to repair itself, rather than powering down for good.

'Stuart,' Billy said.

The cop turned, saw Billy, turned back. Shook his head.

Billy put a hand on the cop's shoulder.

'I'm so sorry,' he said.

The cop sighed. 'You found her?'

Billy nodded.

'This isn't right,' the cop said.

Billy indicated Martha. 'Stuart, this is Martha, she works at the paper.'

Martha didn't speak. What could she say? Nothing was appropriate for a man sitting by the bed of an attempted suicide in a coma. She knew that from bitter experience.

'Martha, this is Stuart, DI Price, Rose's . . .'

He didn't need to say who this man was to Rose, it was obvious.

'Describe the scene for me,' Stuart said.

'Are you sure?'

Stuart nodded.

Billy ran through it – the booze, the pills, Rose on the bed. Seemed more normal in the retelling, less life and death, somehow, just another everyday suicide attempt.

Stuart rubbed at his temple. 'Doesn't make sense.'

'I know,' Billy said.

'This isn't like Rose at all.'

Billy just nodded. Martha supposed there was a limit to the number of times you could say 'I know'. And their job wasn't to fill the space, it was to let Stuart talk it out.

Martha remembered something. 'The laptop.'

'What?' Stuart said.

'Rose's laptop was open on the bed, as if she'd been working on it.'

Billy's eyebrows were raised. 'That's right, I forgot about it in all the madness.'

Stuart's eyes widened. 'We need to get that laptop right now.'

Martha undid the buckles on her bag and pulled it out. 'I picked it up, thought it might be useful.'

Stuart and Billy gave each other a look that made Martha feel good.

'But it's password-protected.' She opened it up. 'Any ideas?'

Billy nodded. 'I know it. "Jeanjeanie".'

Stuart nodded.

Billy took the laptop and typed in the password. The screen lit up and they all stared at it. An open Word document, a few lines typed:

I'm sorry.

For a long time I have kept a secret. Their are terrible things in my past, things I shouldn't have done, things I feel so guilty about. I have wronged someone so badly, and I have taken away the best years of his life as a result.

I don't want sympathy. I am a bad person. I can't live with what I've done. Sorry to everyone I've hurt. Goodbye.

'Christ,' Stuart said.

'Rose didn't write that,' Billy said.

Stuart looked at him. 'What?'

Billy pointed at the screen. 'She would never make that mistake. "Their" instead of "There"'.

Stuart narrowed his eyes. 'Not even drunk and on pills?'

Billy's mouth was a thin line. 'Trust me, Rose would not make that mistake.'

'So someone else wrote this?' Stuart said.

'Johnny,' Martha said.

'Who?'

She told him everything.

Started with her dad's suicide, her first day in the office, Gordon's call, Ian's journal, Carstairs, the Royal Edinburgh, and now Rose.

All apparently linked by one thing.

Johnny Lamb.

'But why would he be behind this?' Stuart said.

'Good question,' Billy said. 'We tried to get a look at the court report of the incident we found in the paper all those years ago, but the reports that far back are archived, we have to wait a week to hear anything.'

Stuart nodded. 'I'll get it sooner. And I'll dig out the police file as soon as I'm back in the office. We need to find this guy.'

'That's what we've been trying to do,' Martha said.

'What's the last known address?'

Martha shook her head. 'Drummond Street, but he's not staying there.'

'How do you know?'

'Because I'm staying there.'

'Since her house burnt down,' Billy said.

Stuart scratched at the back of his hand and stared at Martha. 'Your house burnt down?'

'Yeah.'

'An accident?'

Martha shrugged. 'I don't know.'

Billy closed the laptop. 'You think Johnny might've had something to do with that?'

That had never occurred to Martha. She'd presumed it had been her. The blanket. The fireplace.

Short-term memory loss. But maybe she hadn't destroyed her home after all.

Stuart frowned. 'It's my job to investigate things. Keep all possibilities open.'

He stood up. Leaned over the bed and kissed Rose on the forehead. 'I'll be back soon, love.'

He turned to Martha and Billy. 'I'll be in touch,' he said, then walked out the room.

Martha looked at Rose. Her skin was oily, like she was encased in a sheen of poison. Martha thought back to their meeting outside the hospital, when she came to see Gordon. Rose had said that Martha reminded her of herself when she was young. She wondered if this fate awaited her when she was older.

But she wasn't going to reach fifty, lying in a hospital bed in a coma, tubes leading out of her. She had a sudden overwhelming feeling she was going to die soon.

CHAPTER 45

It didn't feel right being back in the office.

She should be out searching for Johnny, not cutting and pasting, writing picture captions. But she had to keep in with the paper, had to keep reminding herself this was her big break. Foot in the door and all that. And anyway, she had no idea where to begin looking for Johnny, that was the sad truth.

'How you doing, Fluke?' V said.

News of Rose had spread around the office already. Of course, why wouldn't it? There was genuine concern on V's face. Martha wanted to explain, but really, what did she know for certain? People were suddenly killing themselves around her, maybe that's all there was to it. Maybe this whole Johnny Lamb thing was in her head, she needed a bogeyman to pin everything on, to take away from the awful realisation that some people just can't handle it and want to end it all.

She had a splitting headache. She wondered about the ECT, if it was a delayed side effect.

'I'm fine,' she finally said.

She dug some co-codamol out her bag. V handed

235

her a protein shake to wash them down. She took it and glugged. Horrible.

'Anything I can do, sweetheart?' V said.

Martha shook her head.

'I guess we just have to get on with shit, huh?'

Martha shrugged. Yeah, get on with things. Just keep putting one foot in front of the other and hope you don't walk straight into an open grave, waiting for your sad and lonely little body. Just keep breathing and walking and talking and try not to accidentally shoot yourself in the face, or jump off a high bridge, or take a whole bottle of pills, or slit your wrists or jump in front of a train or stab yourself in the heart over and over again until there was nothing left but meaty mush.

Just get on with it.

She looked at the pile of stuff on her desk. V had helped, printing out likely targets for commissioning out obits over the next few days, making a note of people to call and chat to, freelancers to chase up, one piece of syndicated copy from the States to be edited and laid out on the page.

Truth be told, V had done most of it already, just one or two smaller pieces to write. That was up to Martha, mopping up the minnows, writing about the people no one else thought worthy of attention, shining a torch on the everyday lives of the faceless masses.

She looked at the top sheet of paper in the pile.

Beverley Shields, died peacefully in a hospice yesterday at a ripe old age. She had spent forty years as a nursery teacher in Duddingston. Just along the road from Martha's house.

She thought of her house, a charcoaled shell.

This woman had done nothing amazing, she hadn't travelled around the world, or been part of the fucking Bloomsbury set, or flown across the Atlantic single-handed in a balloon, or spent weeks behind enemy lines gathering intelligence. She had just gone in to work every single day with a smile on her face, teaching three- and four-year-olds how to count, how to behave, how to go to the toilet themselves, and remember to wash their little hands. She had done this for four decades, however many generations that was, and in the same place, so she must've seen kids that she'd taught in the seventies coming back years later as worried parents with their kids, or even grandparents with grandkids, all the while taking a simple pleasure in doing something good for society.

That was a life worth documenting.

Martha couldn't see the piece of paper in her hand, her eyes blurry with tears.

'Why don't you let me do that?' V said.

Martha sniffed and swiped at her eyes with her sleeve. 'It's OK, I've got it.'

V pointed at the screen. 'The transcript's in the usual folder.'

V had already interviewed the woman's daughter. More than enough to fill the three-hundred-word slot they had left. Three hundred words was an insult. Beverley Shields deserved a whole book to herself, a whole fucking library.

We all deserve our own book, an account of how we live our lives, but we never get it. The only people who get written about are either famous bastards or selfish show-offs. Martha wanted to make Beverley front-page news. Look at this woman, look at what she did for everyone, how she lived, how her family and friends all miss her like crazy, how she left a tiny but indelible mark on the universe.

Martha sighed. She began sifting through the transcript, cutting and pasting, shaping it into a narrative. Stripping the extraneous language, the repetitive stuff, the incidental meanderings.

Three hundred words.

Done.

She opened up the page, ready to run the copy in. Stopped.

The obit above was for Gordon Harris.

Another three-hundred-worder.

Byline was 'Virginia Tyler'.

Martha looked across.

'I thought I'd better handle that one,' V said.

Martha read it. It put a nice gloss on his life. No mention of the manner of death, of course, not the done thing. Made him out to be a quiet and reserved character, but a good guy, just getting on with things. And of course, his job as obit writer. V had played up the empathy for the grieving and bereaved angle. Didn't go over the top, make him out to be a saint or anything, just a stand-up guy, living his life.

Until he died.

'Good job,' Martha said.

'Thanks.'

'You have a caring, considerate side after all.'

V smiled. 'Don't go spreading that about, Fluke, or I'll crush you.'

Martha wondered again what her own obit would be like.

'Will you write my obit when I die?' she said to V.

'Honey, I'll be long gone by the time you die.'

'I'm not so sure,' Martha said.

The phone rang.

Martha remembered the first time that had happened with her sitting here at the desk. The start of all this.

She breathed in and out heavily, then closed her eyes. Picked up the phone.

'The *Standard* obituary desk.'

'Sis?'

'Cal.' She unclenched her teeth.

'How's it going?'

'Shit.'

'How shit?'

Of course, he didn't know about Rose yet. 'You wouldn't believe me if I told you.'

'Well, I have some news that might cheer you up a bit.'

'It better be good.'

'I've just been speaking to Mum.'
'I'm not cheered yet.'
'She wants to talk.'
'Still not happy.'
'About Uncle Johnny.'
'OK, you got me.'

CHAPTER 46

A man and a woman wearing those white plastic onesies were on their hands and knees in the living room when Martha and Cal turned up.

Elaine was standing in the front garden, watching through the open window frame as they worked. They had a toolbox open on the floor between them, and they were putting samples into clear plastic bags, writing on the labels of the bags. Systematic, methodical.

They weren't going to miss anything, Martha thought.

Cal went and put an arm around Elaine. She gave a sad smile and touched his hand with hers.

Martha stood beside them.

'You wanted to talk?' she said to Elaine.

Cal gave her a look. 'Just go easy.'

The forensics were heading from the door towards the fireplace. There was no colour in the room, everything now just black and white and grey, their whole lives laid out in monochrome.

'Maybe we should go somewhere else,' Cal said softly.

Elaine shook her head. 'Where else can we go? This is our home. I want to stay here.'

'There isn't even anywhere to sit down, Mum.'

Martha looked around. The sun had disappeared behind Arthur's Seat but the sky was still bright. One of those occasional Scottish spring evenings, bursting with possibilities for the summer, promises that were never fulfilled. The light was making the leaves on the trees across in Figgate Park shimmer.

Martha looked at her feet. Their little square of front lawn needed cutting. Stupid to think of that, when your whole house had gone up in flames, but that's what came to her.

She could still smell the house, the destruction of it.

The forensics were at the fireplace now, poking amongst the ash and dust.

She turned to Elaine. 'So tell us about Johnny Lamb.'

She got another look from Cal, ignored it.

Elaine nodded. 'You deserve to know the truth.'

Martha had her hands on her hips. 'Wow, after twenty years, thanks for that.'

Cal shook his head. 'That's not helping.'

Martha twitched her nose in disapproval.

Elaine didn't turn to look at Cal or Martha, just kept staring at the forensics pair shuffling along on their knees through the ashes.

'The truth is, I never told you about Johnny because I tried to put all that stuff out of my mind. It was a difficult time. You have to understand, we were all very young. You do all sorts of stupid stuff when you're . . .'

'Our age?' Martha said.

Elaine nodded. 'Exactly.'

Cal rubbed Elaine's shoulder. 'Why not start at the beginning, Mum?'

Elaine raised a hand to her forehead, like a cheap psychic pretending to get a message from beyond the grave.

'I met Ian in the Southern Bar on Clerk Street, did you know that?'

She was talking as much to herself as to them.

'The night Nirvana played there. He was cute and funny and interesting. We hit it off straight away. He was already working at the *Standard*, doing work experience as a student.' She glanced at Martha. 'He would've been very proud of you, you know.'

She turned away. 'I thought we were in love. I suppose everyone does at that age. But there was always something at the back of my mind, something nagging away at me, that he wasn't as into the whole thing as I was. I tried not to think about it, I didn't want to be one of those paranoid girl-friends. We were smoking a lot of weed at the time, that didn't help.'

Martha and Cal exchanged a look.

Elaine smiled. 'You didn't know that about your ancient mother, did you? I used to smoke skunk and weed, and take speed too. And drink like a fish.'

'What happened to you?' Martha said. She couldn't help a note of sarcasm coming into her voice.

Elaine looked at her. 'I got old, Martha. And you will one day too.'

'Doesn't mean you have to become completely numb. You totally shut yourself down.'

Elaine looked away again. 'I had good reason for that.'

'Look, I thought you were going to tell us about Johnny?'

Elaine sighed. 'Ian was sleeping with a woman from the office. I knew it, but I never said anything. That's why I slept with Johnny, to get back at Ian.'

'You slept with your boyfriend's brother?' Martha said.

'Don't you judge me,' Elaine said.

'Why didn't you just leave Ian?' Cal said.

'Good question,' Elaine said. 'I ask myself that a lot. But things were confused, complicated. After the incident with Johnny, that night, it didn't really matter.'

'Wait, what fucking incident?' Martha said. 'Is this to do with what happened on North Bridge in '92?'

Elaine's head snapped round. 'How do you know about that?'

Martha just stared at her.

'What do you know?' Elaine said.

'What should I know? Were you there?'

Elaine nodded. 'We were all there.'

'Who's we?'

'Me, Johnny, Ian. Gordon too.'

'You mean Gordon Harris?'

'Yes. And the woman Ian was sleeping with, Rose.'

Martha's eyes widened. 'Wait, Rose Brown?'

Elaine frowned and nodded.

'Jesus Christ,' Martha said. 'Ian was fucking Rose? She was the other woman?'

'Yes.'

'Elaine, Rose is in a coma. She apparently tried to kill herself this morning. Only a few days after Gordon did the same thing. And Johnny is on the loose. What the fuck happened that night?'

Elaine looked confused. 'What do you mean, Johnny is on the loose? You said before that he was in the Royal Edinburgh.'

'Ian signed him out three days before he went off North Bridge. Elaine, this stinks – what the hell is going on?'

Elaine brought her hands up to her face. 'Oh my God, I can't . . .'

Martha grabbed her arms, shook her. 'Yes you can, tell us.'

Cal tried to prise Martha's hands away. 'Hey, that isn't helping.'

'Fuck you.'

Cal separated them and pushed Martha away.

Elaine was crying into her hands.

Martha pointed at her. 'I swear to God, Elaine, you better tell me what the fuck is going on here.'

Martha's phone rang in her pocket. She glared at Elaine for a few seconds, Cal shaking his head in between them, then she pulled out her phone.

Billy. She pressed Answer.

'Not a good time, Billy.'

He was on the move, out of breath.

'Rose is awake,' he said.

CHAPTER 47

She felt like she was living in hospitals these days. Might as well move in, she didn't have a home to go to any more.

Billy was waiting outside the main entrance holding a bunch of flowers.

'You shouldn't have,' Martha said.

'Very funny,' Billy said.

'No, I mean you shouldn't have bought lilies. They're for dead people.'

'There are rules about flowers?' He was already walking and pointing. 'She's in ward nineteen, apparently, this way.'

Took them ten minutes to find her through the corridors and double doors.

They pitched up in a sunny ward mostly full of old people, six to a room.

She was in the bed closest to the window.

Her skin was waxy, the pills still oozing out her system.

'Rose,' Billy said.

She turned and managed a thin smile. 'Billy.'

He leaned in and kissed her, put the flowers on the table next to the bed.

Rose chuckled. 'Lilies are for dead people,' she said.

'So Martha tells me. Sorry.'

Rose turned to Martha and raised her eyebrows.

'Hey,' Martha said, shuffling her weight. 'You OK?'

Rose nodded then looked out the window. Getting dark now, but still a trace of blue at the edge of the world. 'I thought they always gave the bed nearest the window to the one who was going to die next. Not a good sign.'

She laughed, more of a cough than anything, then turned back to Billy. 'You two are quite the little double act. You make a cute couple.'

'Never mind that,' Billy said. 'Just relax.'

Rose's movements were tentative, she was clearly in a lot of pain. She looked at a glass tumbler next to the flowers. 'Can you pass me that water?' she said.

Billy obliged.

Martha watched. Rose had had the stuffing knocked out of her, that was for sure. Martha wondered if she'd had one of those life-affirming epiphanies you were always hearing about. A brush with death making you treasure every moment of life – blah-de-blah.

'Thanks,' Rose said, after a nervous sip. 'I believe I have you two to thank for saving my life.'

'It was Billy, really,' Martha said. 'He was amazing.' The words surprised her as they left her mouth. 'He got your stomach empty and kept you going until the ambulance arrived.'

Billy looked at her. 'Well we wouldn't have been there at all if Martha hadn't seen your name on Johnny Lamb's file at the Royal.'

Rose looked at Martha.

Johnny Lamb, the elephant in the room, Martha thought. The big, lumbering elephant in every fucking room she'd walked into in the last week, it felt like.

Martha pointed at Rose laid out in the hospital bed. 'Johnny did this, right?'

Rose nodded.

Billy put a hand on top of Rose's. 'You don't have to tell us just now.'

'Yes she does,' Martha said.

Rose smiled. 'You're right, of course I do.'

She pushed herself up in bed with careful, difficult movements.

'You OK?' Billy said.

She brushed away his concern with a tiny flick of a wrist, taking her hand away from his.

'He turned up at my front door, just like that,' she said. 'This morning. If this is the same day, is it?'

Billy nodded.

'I wasn't even dressed. I was drinking tea and looking out the window. Beautiful skies this morning. Then the buzzer went. Johnny. After twenty years. He had a gun.'

She stopped for a moment. 'I've never had a gun pointed at me. It doesn't look too bad on television and in films, but something strange comes over you when it really happens. I was paralysed to begin with. He pushed in and took over. Began ordering me about. He seemed calm, though. Like it was just a bit of business. We went to the bedroom and he tried to get me to take the whole bottle of my Xanax. I snapped out of it and refused. He hit me. But he was careful, punches to the body, nothing that would show straight away.'

Her voice was wavering.

'It's OK,' Billy said.

'Eventually he pinned me down and put the gun . . . up me.' She turned away. 'Said he was going to blow my insides to pieces if I didn't take the pills.'

Martha looked down at her feet. Heard Rose crying.

'So I took them. He had gin to wash it down. I drank it.'

Rose wiped at her face.

'Then he relaxed. Just waited. Obviously, he wanted it to look like suicide. I felt groggy. He was standing over me. That's the last I remember until an hour ago.'

Martha swallowed. 'Why's he doing this, Rose?'

'What's the oldest motive in the world?'

Martha looked her in the eye. 'Revenge? For all those years locked up?'

'Bingo.'

'Did he kill Ian and Gordon for the same reason?'

'I don't know for sure, but I think so.'

Martha came over and touched the bed next to Rose's hand.

'Jesus, what happened that night?'

Rose sighed. 'I hadn't thought about Johnny Lamb in years until a couple of weeks ago. When Ian was found dead under North Bridge, it brought everything back.'

'You know Ian was my dad,' Martha said.

Rose frowned. 'Billy told me.'

'So,' Martha said. 'That night?'

'It was Teenage Fanclub,' Rose said.

'The band?' Martha thought of Ian's cassettes. 'What do they have to do with it?'

'That was the gig we were all at,' she said. 'It was a disaster. Not the band, they were great. But the atmosphere was poisonous because of what had been going on for months beforehand.'

'You mean you sleeping with Ian, and Elaine sleeping with Johnny?'

Martha's phone rang, breaking the spell.

'Fuck,' she said.

She took it out her pocket. Elaine. She stared at it for a moment. A long moment. Then finally pressed Answer.

'Martha?' It was a man's voice. A familiar voice. The guy who had phoned her at the office and hung up.

'Yes.'

'If you want to see your mum alive one last time, come to North Bridge right now.'

CHAPTER 48

The taxi turned onto North Bridge and Martha saw the flashing lights.

'Stop at the cop car,' Billy said, digging money out.

The taxi driver spoke over his shoulder. 'Looks like another jumper, eh?'

'Jesus,' Martha said.

They hadn't even closed the road, that's what struck her. Life-or-death stuff going on here, and people were still getting on and off buses, heading to the pub or home from work.

A police car and an ambulance were parked in the bus lane halfway up the road. Martha knew exactly what was below that part of the bridge. Platform 8.

The best place to die.

A female cop ushered pedestrians off the pavement, round the bus lane, then on their way. A few people had stopped to watch, which was clearly annoying the cop.

A male cop was standing talking to two people sitting on the wide spread of wall on the edge of the bridge. Two other cops were standing at the police car, one on the radio. A couple of para-medics hovered at the back of the ambulance, waiting. Wouldn't be much use up here if the jumpers went over. Should be down below, surely?

Billy threw a tenner at the driver as Martha jumped out, the taxi still moving. She stumbled as she hit the ground, then found her feet again.

'Just go around,' the cop said, waving her arms.

Martha shook her head. 'I think that's my mum.'

She couldn't see clearly, it was dark now, just the fizz of streetlights. The small pools of light didn't extend to the wall of the bridge.

The cop looked at Martha and Billy, then turned. 'Jim?'

The cop standing next to the couple on the wall came over.

'Says she's the woman's daughter.'

The cop took her elbow. 'Come on.'

Billy followed. 'I'm with her.'

The woman shrugged and went back to waving her arms at passers-by.

Martha ran over to the wall.

Elaine was crying. She was sitting on the wall, facing out over the ledge, held in a tight grip around the neck by a tall, gaunt man who had a gun pointing into her side. He looked like Ian, but taller, broader. More handsome, but a wild look on his face.

'You made it,' he said.

'Johnny,' Martha said.

'Correct.' Johnny looked behind Martha. 'And this must be Calvin?'

'No, I'm Billy.'

Johnny looked at Martha. 'Who the fuck is Billy?'

'A friend.'

A voice from behind them. 'What the hell?'

Martha turned. 'This is Cal,' she said, as Cal ran past the cop to join them.

'Good, good,' Johnny said. 'All the family together at last, eh?'

He laughed. It was about as far from a happy sound as Martha had ever heard.

Cal edged towards the two of them. 'Just let her go, you fuck.'

'Take it easy, big guy.' Johnny pushed the gun into Elaine's back and she let out a cry then a whimper that made Cal stop.

Johnny turned to the cop.

'You, get over to the car.'

'I can't do that, sir.'

Johnny pointed the gun in his face. 'You can if you don't want me to begin shooting everyone on this bridge, starting with you.'

The cop put his hand out. 'Just stay calm, sir.'

'I bet it's killing you, calling me sir, am I right?'

There was something manic about Johnny. Something loose. Martha wondered how the hell he was ever released. Had he been like this for twenty years?

254

She turned to the cop. 'Shouldn't you be doing something about this?'

He shrugged. 'Waiting on CIT.'

'CIT?'

'Crisis intervention team. They're the experts.'

Martha shook her head. 'Fuck's sake.' She turned to Johnny. 'Please let Elaine go.'

Johnny shook his head.

'Whatever this is about, we can sort it out,' Martha said. She was disgusted at the sound of her own voice, so unconvincing. Pathetic. If she were Johnny, she wouldn't listen either.

'Oh, we're going to sort it out, all right,' Johnny said.

Cal shook his head. 'You need help.'

Johnny laughed again, bitter and nasty. 'I've had all the fucking help I can take, thank you very much.'

He turned to Elaine. 'Why don't you tell them why we're all here?'

Elaine was a wreck, tears and snot on her face.

Johnny grabbed the back of her hair and forced her head forwards so that she was looking out over the drop down to the station. She yelped. He yanked her head backwards.

'Tell them,' he said. 'Tell them what you all did to me that night.'

'We didn't do anything, Johnny,' Elaine said. 'You did it to yourself.'

'You fucking liar.' He rabbit-punched her in the side of the head.

Cal, Martha and Billy took a step forward.

Johnny relaxed and pointed the gun at them. 'Stop.'

Martha had her hands out, pleading. 'Look, we know what you've done, but we can help.'

'You know what I've done?' Johnny looked round. 'What I've done? Really? Why don't you enlighten us all with your pearls of wisdom.'

Martha just wanted to keep him talking. As long as they were talking, no one was jumping or shooting.

'You killed your brother, right here.'

Johnny shook his head. He made a sound that might even have been a tut. 'And you call yourself a journalist, can't even get your facts straight.'

Martha frowned. 'How do you know anything about me?'

Johnny smiled. 'It's the twenty-first century, it's all just a mouse click away. Very different world to the one I knew when I went away.'

'But you did kill Ian here,' Martha said.

'That's where you're wrong,' Johnny said. 'I brought him here. But he jumped of his own free will.'

'With your gun pointing at him?'

'I don't expect you to believe me,' Johnny said. 'But I know it's the truth.'

'Why would he jump?' Martha said.

'Guilt. Shame. Depression. The usual. You know all about it.'

Martha looked round at the cop, who just raised

his eyebrows. She turned back to Johnny. 'Guilt over what?'

'You're the reporter, you figure it out.'

'You being locked up in Carstairs.'

'Correct. Twenty-one fucking years. My whole adult life. You've no idea.'

'They must've had a reason to keep you in there.'

Johnny was shaking his head, as if he didn't want to listen.

'And they were right,' Martha said. 'As soon as you got out, you killed Ian and Gordon.'

Johnny seemed close to tears now. 'I didn't kill Ian. I told you.'

'But you did kill Gordon.'

Johnny stared right through them, as if remembering. He nodded. 'I think he wanted it though. Deep down. I know he did. He just needed a little help to go through with it. Same with Rose.'

Billy spoke. 'Rose isn't dead, we've just come from speaking to her in hospital.'

Johnny considered this for a moment and seemed to deflate. 'Fuck, that's annoying.'

'Why did you try to make them look like suicides?' Martha said, just to keep him talking.

Johnny shook his head. 'Why do you think? I didn't want the police chasing after me while I still had a job to do.'

Martha waved a hand at the police car behind her. 'You've kind of blown that whole suicide thing now, haven't you?'

Johnny looked where she was pointing, then at Elaine. 'It doesn't matter any more, I'm finished. Elaine's the last one. This is the end.'

'Tell us what this is about and we can help you,' Martha said.

Johnny pointed the gun at Elaine, tears on his cheeks. 'Can you believe I was in love with this woman?'

That laugh again, it made Martha shiver.

'I suppose it was a long, long time ago, but I was in love. Even though she was going out with that idiot brother of mine, despite the fact he was fucking Rose.' He turned to speak to Elaine. 'You should've finished with Ian as soon as you found out you were pregnant with my babies.'

The earth shifted under Martha's feet. 'What?'

Johnny nodded. 'Tell them how you've been lying to the two of them for their entire lives.'

Elaine just sat there sobbing. She moved her head, but Martha couldn't tell what she meant.

'Mum?' It was Cal next to her.

Elaine still didn't speak.

'Just call me Daddy,' Johnny said.

'Elaine?' Martha's voice sounded weird in her own ears. 'Is this true?'

Silence for a moment, no sign of anything from Elaine.

'That's bullshit and you know it,' Cal said.

'Is it?' Johnny said. 'Think about it. I've had quite the eye-opening chat with Elaine today. We've had a little while to catch up, finally. Seems like you pair have inherited my brain problems, right?'

Cal shook his head. 'We've inherited nothing from you. We're just ourselves, neither you nor Ian ever gave us anything.'

Martha wished it were as simple as that. She wished she could just dismiss the idea, could strike a line through her past and start afresh. But every time the depression descended, she was reminded of her heritage, wherever it came from.

She looked around again. The cop was on his radio. Where the fuck were these crisis experts? Elaine was shaking and crying. The gun was still dug into her ribs and Johnny had a strong grip on her hair with his other hand.

Cal spoke. 'Why did you burn down our house?'

'What?'

'Whatever happened that night twenty years ago has got nothing to do with me and Martha,' Cal said. 'So why the fuck did you burn our house down?'

Johnny looked confused. 'I didn't.'

'Come on,' Cal said. 'You've admitted killing Gordon and trying to kill Rose. What's a little arson compared to that?'

Johnny seemed to make a decision. 'Fuck it, I've had enough of this.'

He stood up on the wall and pulled Elaine to her feet, then he jumped down onto the stone ledge on the other side, hauling Elaine with him.

For a brief moment they both lost their balance, and Martha thought they were going to go over. She ran to the wall, Billy and Cal at her side, all three of them reaching out.

But Johnny wasn't falling. He'd righted himself, and he was pointing the gun at them. He had Elaine in a headlock.

'I'm going to do what I tried to do twenty years ago,' he said. 'Only this time I'm going to get it right.'

'We're not going to let you jump,' Cal said.

Johnny turned to Elaine. 'He's a chip off the old block, eh?'

'You don't know anything about us,' Cal said. 'You're nothing to do with us.'

'I wasn't allowed to be,' Johnny said. 'Thanks to her and Ian, and the rest.'

'You think this is a game of happy families?' Cal said.

As Johnny was talking with Cal, Martha had been inching nearer. Watching Johnny closely. Getting ready to move. Johnny was waving the gun around to make a point, which meant it wasn't aiming at Elaine any more.

'You're missing the point,' Johnny said. 'I don't want happy families. In fact, quite the opposite. I wasn't allowed it, so no one else gets it either.'

He took a small step backwards, to the edge of the ledge, dragging Elaine with him.

Elaine struggled to pull away, but Johnny had her tight.

'I just wanted you both here to see this,' he said. 'So your lives could be ruined just like mine was.'

He lifted the gun momentarily to make a saluting gesture.

Martha jumped onto the wall and grabbed his gun arm, yanking it away from his body in an attempt to shake the gun loose. She saw Cal out the corner of her eye scrabble to get hold of his other arm, prise it away from Elaine's neck. Billy was up on the wall too, then suddenly over, on the ledge. He headbutted Johnny, flattened his nose in a spray of blood. Johnny reeled backwards just as Cal wrenched his grip free from Elaine.

Martha was still holding his gun arm and being dragged over the edge as Johnny's balance deserted him, his momentum sending him backwards, hovering for an impossible second with a blank look in his eyes.

No panic, no anger.

Just blank.

Martha's hold on his sleeve slipped, she felt the material under her fingers as it tore away, and she made an instinctive grab for him.

But he was already gone, tumbling downwards, arms and legs flailing.

He hit platform 8 with a heavy whump that Martha felt in her bones.

She felt a hand pull her back from the ledge and turned to see Billy holding onto her from behind.

Beside him, Cal had Elaine in a bear hug, leaning against the wall, both of their chests heaving.

She turned to look at Johnny's body again.

No movement.

He almost looked like he was sleeping.

GIG #4, 12/9/92

Her life was such a fucking mess, even the Fanclub playing 'The Concept' couldn't cheer her up.

The Music Box was heaving, sweat dripping from the ceiling. It was a dingy, stinking place anyway, but it felt like the walls were closing in on her. She felt dizzy and sick. She gripped the gig ticket in her fist, stared at it, trying to focus, make her breathing steady:

REGULAR MUSIC LTD
presents
TEENAGE FANCLUB
at THE MUSIC BOX, EDINBURGH
Saturday 12 September, doors 10 pm
Ticket £6 plus booking fee

On stage, Norman was singing, 'She don't do drugs, but she does the pill, oh yeah.' If only Elaine had been more like the girl in the song.

She didn't know why they called it morning sickness, she got it all hours of the day and night. She looked at her watch. It was after midnight, and she felt another wave of nausea sweep over her. What was she even doing here? Trying to convince Ian and herself that everything was OK, everything was normal, everything was going to be fine.

But it wasn't.

She was living a lie. Her relationship with Ian was over, it's just that no one had done anything to actually finish it yet.

Tonight felt like the end point though. This couldn't go on any longer.

She sipped her lager. Shouldn't be drinking, but she hadn't told anyone yet, and didn't want Ian to guess. Not until she'd worked out what the hell she was going to do.

So she was drinking and smoking joints and hiding her sickness and swollen ankles. That was easy to hide, Ian was barely interested in her anyway, they hardly ever fucked any more.

He was too busy fucking Rose.

Not that Elaine had any proof, or any moral high ground. She'd been fucking Johnny on and off since that first time in June.

And now she was pregnant.

But Johnny wasn't the answer, he was getting weirder. Really intense. Scaring her by talking about a future together one minute, then about how much he wanted to hurt himself the next, how there was no point to anything. Too much drama. How could she possibly ditch Ian and make a life with Johnny?

She couldn't see a way out.

She felt a nudge. Ian beside her. She gave him a thin smile.

'It's your round,' he said. He glanced at her pint. 'You're going a bit slow, eh? What's up?'

'Nothing.'

She headed to the bar.

The band played 'Star Sign' and the crowd went ape. She couldn't handle a fast one. Gerry was singing lead this time. 'Do you know where you belong?' If only.

She ordered a Stella for Ian.

'Hey gorgeous.' She felt arms around her and squirmed free.

Johnny.

She pushed him away. 'What the hell are you doing here?'

'That's a nice way to greet your lover.' He drawled the last word stupidly, like he was making a joke of it. It wasn't a joke.

'Ian is just over there,' Elaine said. 'Jesus Christ, did you follow us?'

Johnny held his hands up. 'Hey, just enjoying a bit of the Fannies, no crime in that, is there?'

'Go home, Johnny.'

He went to kiss her and she dodged out the way. He grabbed her jaw and forced their lips together.

She pulled back. 'Ow, that fucking hurt.'

'Why haven't you told him about us yet?'

The pint of Stella arrived and Elaine paid.

'It's not as simple as that.'

'Yes it is. Want me to do it?'

Elaine shook her head. 'No.'

'If you don't, I will.'

'Please Johnny, I have to handle this my own way.'

Johnny reached into his jacket pocket and pulled something out. 'Maybe this will help you handle it.'

He handed over a packet of photographs. Elaine opened the flap and squinted at the first one in the neon light from the bar.

Ian and Rose kissing in the street. Holding hands.

She flicked to the next one. Nighttime. The pair of them up against a tree, in the Meadows it looked like, her inner thigh rubbing against his leg, his hand up her blouse.

Picture five, they were fucking against the tree, Ian's trousers and boxers pushed down, Rose's skirt hiked up, her pants at her ankles.

Elaine flicked through the rest of the pictures. Different days, different places, always together, sometimes fucking, mostly snogging or with their hands in each other's pants. They were very tactile in a way she couldn't remember ever being with him.

The last two were of them sitting together in a park, her head on his shoulder, both of them laughing. For some reason this was worse than the pictures of them fucking. They looked like two people in love.

She glared at Johnny. 'You followed them and took pictures?'

'Thought you could use the evidence.'

Elaine shook her head.

Johnny grabbed her elbow, his face too close to hers. The vodka on his breath made her feel sick.

'Don't you see, this gives you the excuse you need.'

She pushed herself free. 'I'm going to be sick.'

She ran to the toilet.

Into a cubicle just in time, felt the puke rushing up her throat, stripping the skin away as her stomach convulsed.

She felt a hand on her back, rubbing.

Johnny. 'It's OK.'

'Get out.'

'We'll go and tell him together,' Johnny said.

Elaine spat into the toilet. 'No, we won't.'

'It's simple.'

'It's not.'

'Why isn't it?'

'Because I'm pregnant.'

It just spilled out and she regretted it straight away.

At least it shut him up for a minute. But only a minute.

'It's mine, isn't it?' he said.

He was too intense, too much was happening far too quickly. She didn't want him to have a hold over her, to have a link to her future.

'I don't know,' she said.

'Don't lie,' he said. 'I know it's mine.'

Elaine pushed past him to the sinks, took a mouthful of water and rinsed her mouth out.

'Go home, Johnny,' she said. 'We'll talk about this tomorrow.'

'No. Now.'

'You're drunk.'

'So what?'

'I can't handle this.'

She left the ladies. The band were playing 'Everything Flows', one of her favourites.

She saw Ian and couldn't believe it. He was standing talking to Rose, Gordon and Sam lurking in the background. Really? Ian and Rose had some balls.

Elaine had to get out of here.

She went to the bar, picked up the pint that she'd bought him, still sitting there, then walked up to Ian and tapped him on the shoulder.

When he turned, she threw the pint in his face, then dropped the plastic glass. Beer sprayed all over Rose, who seemed to be smiling at her. She wanted to punch that smile.

She turned and pushed through the crowd towards the door. She was vaguely aware of Johnny behind her, talking to Ian and the rest.

The band were in the big finale of the song. 'Set a course that I don't know.'

She pushed the door and headed upstairs, claustrophobia drowning her, suddenly needing fresh air above anything else on earth.

She was halfway down the Royal Mile before she heard the voices calling after her.

She didn't turn round, just shook her head and

kept walking. Didn't want to do this now. Didn't want to do it ever, just wanted to go home and sleep until it was all over.

'Elaine.'

Ian.

Or Johnny.

Shit, did it matter?

At the top of Cockburn Street she glanced back. They were all coming, gaining on her. Ian, Johnny. Fucking Rose. Even Gordon, what did it have to do with him? No sign of Sam.

She hit the junction with the Bridges. Taxis and night buses streaming up and down.

Home was to the right, up South Bridge, but Ian and the rest were across the road, coming towards her from that direction.

She went left, onto North Bridge. Needed some space to clear her head.

'Elaine, fuck's sake, wait.' Definitely Ian that time.

She heard an argument. Turned and saw the brothers were scuffling in the road, Gordon trying to separate them. She walked further away, across the road, down North Bridge, anything to get away.

She heard footsteps and knew what was coming. Felt a hand on her shoulder, spinning her.

Rose.

'Wait.' She was out of breath.

'Fuck off.'

'I'm sorry.'

'I said fuck off.' Elaine shook free of Rose's hand

269

but didn't walk away. She looked at her. Rose was puffing, chest heaving. She was so much more of a woman than Elaine, knew all the tricks of capturing male attention. Older, wise to the world.

The boys had caught up.

'You're pregnant?' Ian said. 'Why the hell didn't you tell me?'

She could see everyone was drunker than she was, and she wasn't exactly sober. This was ridiculous. 'I'm not having this conversation now.'

'Why not?' Johnny said.

'Because it's half past fucking midnight, we've all been drinking for hours and I feel sick and want to go home.'

'Just calm down,' Rose said.

'Don't you fucking speak to me,' Elaine said. 'Just don't. I know exactly what you've been doing with my boyfriend, don't you tell me to calm down.'

What was she doing? She didn't want Ian, so why pretend to be angry about this? But it was the betrayal, the deceit.

'And you've been fucking Johnny,' Rose said quietly.

Elaine's eyelids felt very heavy. She scrunched her eyes shut, opened them and looked at Ian.

He didn't doubt it. She could tell from the look on his face that he'd probably known all along, he just hadn't admitted it to himself. How many of us sleepwalk through life, she thought, never telling the truth to ourselves.

270

His face now looked like he'd just woken up from a coma. He was piecing his senses and his life back together.

'Is the baby mine?' he said.

Elaine didn't speak.

Johnny came forward and put a hand on his brother's shoulder. 'Ian . . .'

Ian shook it off. 'I said, is the baby mine?'

It would be easy to say yes or no. Just say yes or no, put an end to this.

Ian looked at Johnny, then back at her. 'How long has this been going on behind my back?'

Johnny pulled the photos from his pocket. 'Don't get on your fucking high horse.'

He handed them to Ian, who opened the packet. Hardly even looked inside.

'You've been following me?'

'With good reason, it turns out,' Johnny said.

'You are fucked up,' Ian said. 'This is Debbie Logan all over again.'

'It's nothing like that.'

Elaine had no idea what they were talking about.

'It's exactly like that. Anything I have, you want. It's pathetic.'

'Anything you have?' Elaine said. 'Excuse me.'

Johnny pushed at Ian. 'You're screwing Rose. At least I was being a friend to Elaine.'

'Calm down.' This was Gordon, trying to get in between them.

Rose had her hand up to her head.

Ian grabbed at his brother, past Gordon. 'A

271

friend? You're such a fuck-up, you probably believe that's true. You're so fucking deranged. I've spent my whole life looking out for you, I've had enough.'

'Deranged?' Johnny said. A strange look came over him. 'I'll show you deranged.'

He leapt up onto the wall of the bridge, then was quickly over the other side, standing on the ledge.

Elaine went to grab his hand. 'Johnny, for fuck's sake.'

He had stopped on the ledge and was looking back, grinning. 'How's this for deranged?'

Ian laughed. 'Oh, here we go.' He shook his head. 'You going to jump, yeah? Show us all how mental you really are?'

'What if I did?'

'Come on,' Ian said. 'That would be suicide bid number, what? Four? Five?'

Elaine stared at Ian. 'What?'

Ian looked at her. 'He's never serious. It's an attention thing. There's fuck all wrong with him. He just likes being a drama queen.'

Elaine reached out over the wall. 'Come on, Johnny, come back over.'

'No, I'm going to do it,' Johnny said. Something in his face made Elaine believe him.

She clambered up onto the wall.

'Hey,' Ian said. 'What are you doing?'

She briefly turned back. 'I'm trying to stop your brother doing something really stupid. It's more than you're doing.'

'It's what he wants,' Ian said. 'It's all about the attention.'

Punters were giving them a wide berth on the pavement. They were just a bunch of drunken nutters dangerously mucking around.

Elaine was sitting on the wall now, reaching out.

'Come on, Johnny, give me your hand.'

She stretched for him, but he shirked away, towards the edge.

'OK, relax,' Elaine said.

Rose spoke. 'Please come back over, Elaine.'

Elaine turned to her. Maybe in other circumstances they could've been friends. But she was fucked if she was going to take advice from the woman, not now.

'Fuck you,' she said.

This was all so messed up. If they could just get down from this bridge and go home, they could sort it all out.

She felt a hand take hers and turned. Johnny. She felt relief, but that changed when she saw his face. He looked in a daze, like he didn't know where he was.

'Come here, you cunt,' Ian said, and made a lunge for Johnny's other arm.

Johnny flinched away and in a quick movement grabbed Elaine and hauled her down onto the ledge. He pulled her into a hug and stepped backwards off the ledge.

'I'm sorry,' he whispered in her ear.

Her feet left the ledge and she felt herself falling,

a sudden blast of air around her as Johnny's grip tightened and they fell together.

The adrenalin made her breath stop as they dropped through the sky, and the last thing she thought before they hit the ground was that Johnny was not only killing himself and her, but the unborn baby sleeping inside her.

CHAPTER 49

The question hung in the air.

Martha stared at Elaine, wondering if she was going to answer.

Eventually Elaine turned and looked her in the eye. A tiny shake of the head.

'The truth is, I don't know,' she said. 'I never found out which one was your dad. Both are possible, if you know what I mean. In the end, does it really matter?'

Martha thought about that. They were both dead now, and neither of them had done much for Martha or Cal when they were alive. Except maybe give them a family history of mental illness. Cheers for that.

Did it really matter?

Elaine glanced round and Martha followed her gaze. Ian's flat looked like it had been turned over, but that was just the state Martha had left it in the previous night.

There had been a second ambulance down below by the time Johnny had fallen onto platform 8, and they were at his body straight away. The police officer up on the bridge got the call on his radio moments later. Dead on impact.

Martha, Cal, Billy and Elaine were checked over by the paramedics up top. No physical problems. They were interviewed by police while sitting on the back step of the ambulance. The crisis intervention team turned up ten minutes too late.

For Martha and the rest there would be follow-up stuff, according to the police, but for now they were free to go, did they have somewhere to stay?

Ian's flat.

'This is where Ian lived?' Elaine said.

Cal nodded.

Billy was pouring out the last of the brandy into mugs. He handed them out and sat down.

Elaine turned to Martha. 'I was in hospital for two months after the fall.'

She had already explained what happened that night. The drunken fight on the bridge, the jump.

'The doctors said it was a miracle you both survived. I only found out I was expecting twins after I came round two days later. Apparently Johnny had cushioned my fall. He was even more badly injured than I was.'

Martha thought about that. A massive trauma like that while still in the womb, that could have an effect on how two babies turned out, couldn't it? Maybe that was the reason she and Cal were the way they were.

Cal went over and touched Elaine's arm. 'So Ian had Johnny committed?'

Elaine sipped her brandy. 'That was all done while I was still in hospital. Ian never came to see me. Gordon kept me up to date on what Ian was doing. Apparently, it wasn't the first time Johnny had tried something like that, not by a long way. Gordon said that during the trial they mentioned five other suicide attempts, one of which also involved a young woman. That time pills, a suicide pact, except the girl didn't know anything about it, woke up in hospital but refused to press charges.'

Martha frowned. 'But even with a history of mental instability, Johnny was in Carstairs for so long.'

Elaine shrugged. 'If you don't show improvement, they can keep you in forever, especially if you still seem a danger to others. The impression I got from Gordon was that Johnny got worse inside there. And since Ian was his only remaining relative, he had a big say in what happened.'

'You think Ian kept him in out of spite?'

'Maybe that was part of it. Maybe he was sick of having to clean up his brother's messes. And Johnny really was a threat, Christ, he's proven that since he came out, hasn't he?'

Martha drank. 'But why do you think Ian changed his mind recently, why sign him out after all these years?'

Elaine shook her head. 'Maybe he felt remorse. Maybe Johnny tricked him. We're never going to know, are we?'

Cal sighed. 'You think it's true, what Johnny said, that Ian jumped of his own accord?'

Elaine didn't answer. There weren't any more answers. She looked down at her mug. 'I'm sorry. I should've told you both about Johnny. And I shouldn't have told you that Ian was your dad when I didn't know for sure. But it just crept up on me. When you were little it wasn't a problem, it was just the three of us. But then you started asking about why you didn't have a daddy, all that stuff. I suppose I panicked a little bit, I just thought it was easier to say Ian. I spoke to him about it, and he said he was fine with it, as long as we didn't expect anything from him. Back when it happened, it was horrible, I didn't want to think about any of it ever again. I was recovering from the fall, on my own, with twins coming. I wanted a fresh start. The three of us. We didn't need a dad. Not Ian or Johnny or anyone else. You understand that, don't you?'

There were big streaks of tears on her face as Cal gave her a hug.

'It's OK,' he said, rubbing her back.

Elaine looked at Martha.

'Martha? You understand why I did it, don't you?'

Martha looked around the room, at Billy, at the mess of her life, at the flat of the man she used to think was her dad. Maybe he still was. Maybe he wasn't. Maybe it didn't matter.

She downed her brandy and sighed.

'I understand.'

CHAPTER 50

'You don't have to do this,' Cal said.

'Yes, I do.'

Back in the ECT waiting room next morning. Same beige and brown walls, same scratchy seats. Martha fiddled with the information leaflet in her hand. Two sessions per week for three weeks. Switching things off and back on again.

She looked at Cal. 'Besides, I think I could do with some short-term memory loss, don't you?'

Cal raised his eyebrows at her.

The door opened and Colleen shuffled through. Big smile when she saw the two of them.

'It's yourselves,' she said. She sorted through some papers on her desk and handed Martha the clipboard and questionnaire. The same one she'd filled in two days ago, how was she feeling, any major stress in the last seven days, all that.

'Did you catch up with that fella you were looking for?' Colleen said to Martha.

Martha and Cal looked at each other and shook their heads.

'We did,' Martha said.

CHAPTER 51

She stood outside the hospital and blinked. Sunlight was fizzing all around her, and she stood there like a lizard on a rock, warming her blood. She was aware of air molecules colliding with her eyeballs, drifting up her nose. She breathed in. Cigarette smoke and pollen and cheap cooking smells. Good to be alive after all.

She looked at her watch. Four hours ago she'd woken up in a different hospital. Took it easy this time, let Cal and the nurse take care of her for a bit. Then she'd sat up and persuaded Cal to let her come here.

She headed inside and followed the signs for ward 19.

Rose was out of bed, sitting in a classy silk nightie in the plastic chair by the window. The view outside was terrible, chunky hospital buildings, air vents, a meat delivery truck down below.

'Hey,' Martha said.

Rose turned and smiled. It was a genuine smile and Martha liked it.

'Hi, Martha,' Rose said. 'Sit down.'

She waved at a seat over by an empty bed.

Martha grabbed it and brought it over, sat across from her.

'Billy has been in,' Rose said. 'Told me everything that happened.'

'Yeah.'

Rose shook her head. 'Quite a night.'

'You could say that.'

'How are you doing?'

Martha did a little inventory. No headaches. No aches and pains. No heavy weight pressing down on her, no blackness on the horizon. Her heart felt light, like it could float on water.

'I'm good.' She rummaged in her bag and pulled out Rose's laptop. 'Here.'

Rose gave her a strange look. 'You hold onto that for now.'

'Why?'

'Do you have your own laptop?'

'No.'

'Well, keep it for me, you can put it to good use. I'm sure you'll need it. Not so sure I'll be doing much writing for a while.'

Martha frowned. 'But you are going back to the paper, right?'

Rose stared out the window. 'We'll see. Maybe.'

'Rose, you have to.'

Rose just shrugged.

Martha laid the laptop on her knees. 'You know he typed a suicide note from you on this.'

'Billy told me about the typo.'

They were both smiling.

Martha put the laptop back in her bag, pulling out the Walkman to make room for it.

Rose looked at it. 'You should probably invest in some new technology, you know.'

Martha passed the cassette player from one hand to the other. 'I quite like this old thing.'

'I'm sure you've got a long career as a reporter ahead of you,' Rose said.

'You think?'

Rose nodded. 'Like I said before, you remind me a lot of myself at your age.'

'I'll take that as a compliment.'

Silence for a moment between them. Rose coughed and held her side, winced. 'How are you and Elaine?' she said.

'How do you mean?'

'Don't be too hard on her, Martha. She did what she thought was best for her children.'

'You think?'

'She loves you and she brought you up OK, didn't she?'

Martha didn't speak. She could feel Rose examining her closely.

'Billy told me where you were this morning,' Rose said.

Martha raised her eyebrows. 'And?'

'Does it work?'

Martha nodded. 'Yeah, it works.'

'Good.'

Martha got up to leave, the Walkman still in her hand.

Rose put a hand out. 'Look after Billy for me, will you?'

Martha smiled. 'He's perfectly capable of looking after himself.'

'Nevertheless, look out for him.'

'I will, Rose.' She took Rose's hand, a firm grip. 'You take it easy now, you hear?'

Rose coughed out a laugh. 'I'll try.'

CHAPTER 52

Her whole body felt shaky as she got off the bus.

Was she just picking at the scab, or was this some half-baked idea about closure?

North Bridge was busy. Rush hour on a Friday, everyone keen to get somewhere. She felt like a twig in a stream, swaying under the influence of everyone around her.

She had her earphones in, listening to another of Ian's cassettes. She looked at the box. It was the B side of the very first tape she'd listened to on the way to the *Standard* offices. That was The Lemonheads, this time The Breeders. *Last Splash.* Sounded weird but cool, two women singing about a cannonball.

She crossed the road to the east side of the bridge, saw the Samaritans' sign, the same one from before. Who cares? We do. We don't.

She walked to the exact spot. Put her hands on the wall. Felt the rough stone under her fingers. Rubbed her hands up and down lightly.

She leaned over and looked down at platform 8.

Busy with commuters, weekend travellers, people heading all sorts of places, away from here.

She thought about that.

The sun was behind her, casting her shadow onto the stone of the bridge. She looked out to sea, just calm blue, a couple of oil tankers, seemingly still. Then she looked at Calton Hill to the left, lit up in the afternoon sunshine.

The Breeders were creepy now in her ears, like it was recorded underwater. She caught a line, 'Raw, where the shot leaves me gagging for the arrow'.

She turned and walked down the bridge, turned right at the junction and up Waterloo Place. Her stride quickened as she went. Took the turning up Calton Hill, through the trees, along the path, bending round and up, round and up.

She reached the top, out of breath, panting, and turned. From here you could see all the way down Princes Street to the castle and past it to the Pentlands. Thousands of people going about their normal day, carrying all the stuff around with them that folk did, each with their story to tell, each one as insignificant as the rest, each one just as important.

North Bridge looked like a little model, toy cars and buses shunting up and down. The distance from North Bridge down to the train platform below looked like nothing, like jumping off a garden wall.

Perspective.

The Breeders were playing 'I Just Wanna Get

Along' in her ears. Chugging surf rock. They sounded like a fun band to have a beer with.

She sat down, opened her bag, pulled the laptop out and opened it on her knees. Powered it up. Looked at the clouds while she waited. Then opened a new document and began typing.

Obituary: Martha Fluke
Born: 14 April 1993, in Edinburgh.
Died: ?? ?? 20??, in ??, aged ??.

Martha Fluke was a highly accomplished and greatly admired journalist. She was born in Edinburgh and studied journalism at Napier University before going on to . . .

She took a deep breath and looked away from the screen. Her mind was blank. She tried to imagine what kind of life she might have, the kind of things a decent obituary writer would put in. She couldn't.

She clicked on Word Count. Twenty-five words so far. That was all she could think of for twenty years of life. Even for a short piece, how would she fill the other 275 words?

She saved the file, closed the screen and stared at North Bridge way down below, feeling the sun on her face.

CHAPTER 53

She scanned the trees looking for her wood pigeon. Or the cat that had brought her the offering before. Nothing.

The cemetery was busy. Gordon had more friends than anyone had realised.

Martha thought about the three-hundred-word obituary they ran yesterday. How many words did it take to sum up a life?

Everyone from the office was here except for Rose, still recovering in hospital.

V looked amazing in a tight trouser suit, high heels and a faded Aerosmith T-shirt under her jacket. Well, at least it was black. She gave Martha a wink from the other side of the grave.

Martha put her arm through Billy's and rested her head on his shoulder.

It seemed like the ECT yesterday had been a success. She still felt great today, far too good to be at a funeral. She almost felt like dancing among the tombstones.

The minister was talking but Martha wasn't listening. She looked at all the faces around the grave, thought about the impact Gordon Harris had made with his short time on earth. Tiny, really, like any of us. But not nothing, that was the main thing.

Sam was sobbing, face puffy, looking afraid and desperate.

Martha wondered what she would be like at her own husband's funeral, if she ever had a husband. Or at Cal's funeral. Or Elaine's.

The tears came. Not for Gordon, or Ian or Johnny. Not for the thought of Cal or Elaine. But for herself, and for everyone else on the planet, trudging along in their day-to-day existence, quietly, heroically living the best life they could manage for as long as they were here.

Billy hugged her closer and squeezed her arm as they lowered the coffin into the ground.

Martha remembered Gordon's face half missing, putting her hand on the carpet soaked in his piss, the ride in the ambulance.

Sam threw a handful of dirt on the coffin, then her legs buckled and she sank to her knees. She was helped up by an older man and led away.

That was the signal for everyone else to break.

Martha wiped at her cheeks and looked up at Billy. Kissed him on the lips.

She turned him away from the graveside and began walking. She wanted to show him.

A hundred yards away she stopped at Ian's grave. Looked around again for the wood pigeon. Nothing.

The grass seed still hadn't taken in the soil. She wondered if it would.

'So this is Ian,' Billy said.

'Yeah.' Martha had a thought. 'Will they dig him up?'

Billy looked at her. 'Why would they do that?'

'Forensics, maybe they can tell whether he jumped or whether Johnny forced him over somehow.'

'Wouldn't they have already done a post-mortem?'

Martha shook her head. 'It's not standard for suicides.'

'If it was suicide.'

'Exactly.'

Elaine and Cal joined them at the grave. Elaine's eyes were red and she was sniffing into a tissue.

'I don't know why I'm crying, I hadn't seen Gordon in two decades.'

Martha nodded at Ian's grave. 'Will they put Johnny next to him?'

Elaine shrugged. 'Do you think they should?'

'I don't suppose it matters.'

Cal looked at Elaine then turned to Martha. 'We've got some news.'

'Yeah?'

'The fire service forensic team have submitted their report.'

Martha closed her eyes. Pictured the living room as it used to be.

'And?'

'Cause of fire is undetermined.'

Martha opened her eyes again. 'What does that mean?'

Elaine spoke. 'It means they don't know why it happened. Whether it was an accident, or whether Johnny did it.'

'More importantly,' Cal said, 'it means the insurance will pay out. So we'll have our home back eventually.'

Martha thought about that. She didn't know if she wanted it back.

'Fluke.'

It was V striding towards them, McNeil in her wake.

V walked up and gave Martha a hug. 'Hey, kiddo.' She broke away and did the same to Billy, then spoke under her breath to both of them, pointing at McNeil behind her. 'Buggerlugs here has some interesting chat for you pair. Be cool.'

'Martha,' McNeil said. 'Billy.' He looked over his shoulder. 'A sad business.' He turned back, shuffled his feet a little. 'Virginia has been filling me in on what you have been up to.'

Martha held onto Billy's arm.

'Rose has handed in her notice,' McNeil said.

'What?' Billy said.

'I've refused it, of course. Still trying to talk her round. Think she just needs some time off.' He waved his hand around the graveyard. 'Anyway, I'll hold her job open as long as she wants, but I need someone to cover for her, which is where you come in. We also, of course, have a permanent vacancy on the obituary desk, if either of you are interested in that.'

He harrumphed and rubbed his hands.

'So, that's it. There are two jobs going, crime reporter and obituary writer. You can take your pick between you. Either way, see you both in the office on Monday, yes?'

V smiled. 'Well?'

Martha and Billy looked at each other for a long time.

'I don't mind,' Billy said, holding his hands out.

Martha looked past him, at the hundreds of graves, hundreds of lives, hundreds of stories that deserved to be told. Sunlight snuck through the oak trees, and she spotted something up there amongst the branches. Her wood pigeon, ruffling its feathers, face turned upwards, soaking up the warmth.

She looked at Billy and smiled.

'I'll take the dead beat,' she said.